THIS DIARY BELONGS TO:

Nikki J. Maxwell

PRIVATE & CONFIDENTIAL

If found, please return to ME for REWARD!

(NO SNOOPING ALLOWED!!!☹)

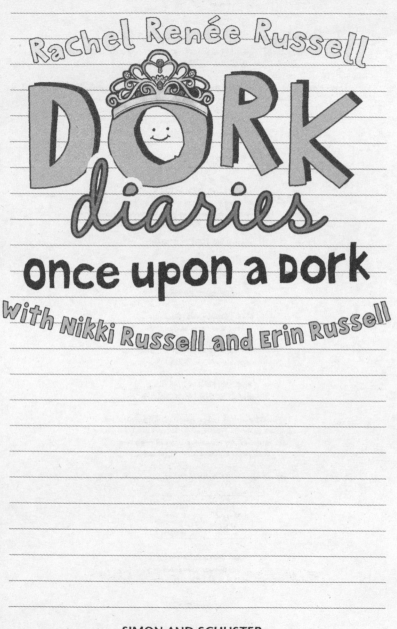

Rachel Renée Russell

DORK diaries

Once upon a Dork

with Nikki Russell and Erin Russell

SIMON AND SCHUSTER

This edition published 2016
First published in Great Britain in 2014 by Simon & Schuster UK Ltd
A CBS COMPANY

First published in the USA in 2014 as *Dork Diaries 8: Tales from a Not-So-Happily Ever After*
by Aladdin, an imprint of Simon & Schuster Children's Publishing Division.

Copyright © 2014 Rachel Renée Russell
Designed by Lisa Vega

13

Simon & Schuster UK Ltd
1st Floor, 222 Gray's Inn Road
London WC1X 8HB

Simon & Schuster Australia, Sydney
Simon & Schuster India, New Delhi

A CIP catalogue record for this book
is available from the British Library.

PB ISBN: 978-1-4711-4383-0
eBook ISBN: 978-1-4711-2279-8

Printed and bound by CPI Group (UK) Ltd, Croydon, CRO 4YY

MIX
Paper from
responsible sources
FSC
www.fsc.org   FSC® C020471

www.simonandschuster.co.uk
www.simonandschuster.com.au
www.dorkdiaries.co.uk

To all of my ADORKABLE fans
around the world—follow your
dreams and you too will find
your Happily Ever After!

Hello UK Dorks!

I'm so happy to be able to write to UK fans of my DORK DIARIES series to say a great big THANK YOU for supporting the series and for embracing Nikki Maxwell and her dorky world!

It means so much to me to know that DORK DIARIES has fans all over the world, and being able to share Nikki's stories with all of you here in the UK is very special indeed. Without you guys supporting the series, I wouldn't be able to do what I love, so thank you, thank you, thank you.

Keep being dorky and special and amazing! And always remember to let your inner dork shine through!

Rachel Renée Russell

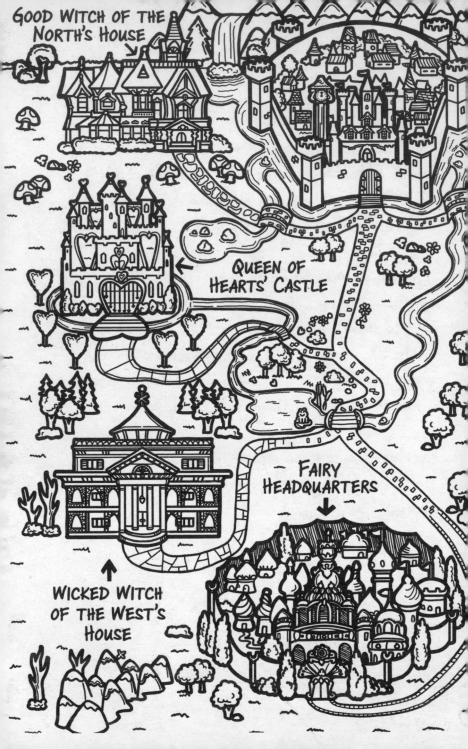

GOOD WITCH OF THE NORTH'S HOUSE

QUEEN OF HEARTS' CASTLE

FAIRY HEADQUARTERS

WICKED WITCH OF THE WEST'S HOUSE

AAAAAAAAAAHHH ☹!!
(That was me screaming in frustration!)

I can't believe I overslept! AGAIN! Now I'm probably going to be late for school! WHY?!! Because my bratty little sister, Brianna, has been sneaking into my bedroom at night and stealing my alarm clock!

She's been using it to get up extra early to make a peanut butter, jelly, and pickle sandwich to take to school for lunch. YES! She actually adds PICKLES!

I don't know which is more NAUSEATING, Brianna or her disgusting sandwich!

Anyway, now I have less than three minutes to shower, shampoo, brush, dress, pack, eat, gloss, and GO!

This is how my very CRUDDY day began. . . .

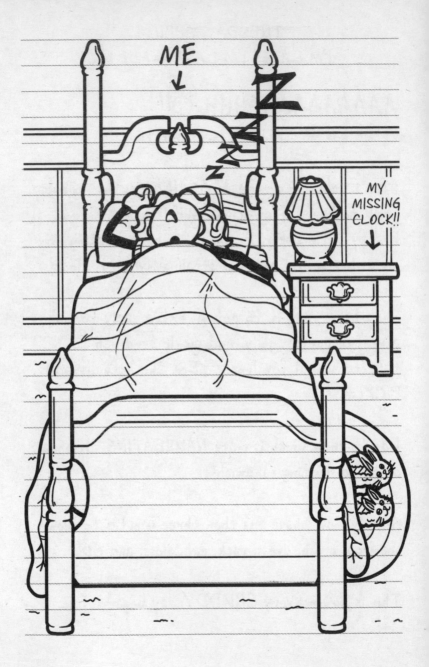

2

WHIRRRR!!

5

HOP!
HOP!

OMG!! I got dressed for school in two minutes and nineteen seconds! Which is probably a NEW late-for-school world record!!

I decided to wear my brand-new sweater with the cool fringe on it. It took me TWO whole months to save up to buy it from SWEET 16, a trendy teen store in the mall.

Looking back on my morning, there was definitely GOOD NEWS and BAD NEWS.

The GOOD NEWS . . . ?

My day had gotten off to such a HORRIBLE start, I was absolutely SURE there was NO WAY things could get any WORSE ☺!

The BAD NEWS . . . ?

I was TOTALLY WRONG about the GOOD NEWS!

☹!!

OMG! I was so TICKED OFF at Brianna for swiping my alarm clock that smoke was practically spewing out of my EARS!! . . .

I wanted to stuff her in a big box and ship her off to Princess Sugar Plum Island to be the pooper-scooper for all those cute little baby unicorns she loves so much.

"Brianna! Did you take my clock again?!" I yelled. "If I'M late for school, it's all YOUR fault!"

"I didn't take your clock. Miss Penelope did! She thinks you need all the BEAUTY SLEEP you can get! Have you looked in the mirror lately?" Brianna said, sticking her tongue out at me.

"Miss Penelope THINKS I need beauty sleep?! Sorry, Brianna, but Miss Penelope CAN'T think. She doesn't have a BRAIN! She's a hand puppet!" I shot back.

"She does TOO have a brain!" Brianna shouted. "She says she can go to puppet school to get smarter, but YOU need to go on that TV show *Ugly Face Intervention!*"

I was like, Oh. No. She. DIDN'T ☹!!! I could NOT believe Miss Penelope was talking TRASH about me like that. SHE was going to need an intervention!! After I took a pen and drew her a mustache. THEN we'd see whose FACE was the most messed up, MINE or HERS!

Anyway, Brianna was at the kitchen table, slopping together peanut butter, jelly, and pickles to make her very disgusting sandwich. . . .

BRIANNA, BUSY MAKING
A DISGUSTING PBJ & P SANDWICH!

"Would you like me to make one for you, Nikki? It's yummy! SEE?" Brianna said, shoving her sandwich right in my face.

I cringed at the slimy, drippy mess. . . .

EWW! It SMELLED even worse than it looked. Kind of like peanut butter, jelly, and, um . . . rancid pickle juice ☹!

"Um . . . no thanks!" I muttered, totally grossed out.

"Come on. Just take one bite!!" Brianna said, waving it under my nose. "You'll LOVE it!"

"No, Brianna! Actually, I'm not hungry anymore! I took one look at your sandwich and COMPLETELY lost my appetite!!"

"Are you SURE? It's awesomely delicious!" She giggled.

I just rolled my eyes at that girl.

What part of the word "NO" did she NOT understand?!

I wanted to scream, Sorry, Brianna, but . . .

I will not eat it with a DOG!
I will not eat it with a FROG!

I will not eat it with a CAT!
I will not eat it with a RAT!

I will not eat it in my ROOM.
On the BUS. Or on the MOON!

I will not eat it NORTH or SOUTH!
It made me throw up in my MOUTH!

Call me PICKY! Call me FICKLE!
I DON'T like PBJ and PICKLES ☹!!!

Anyway, Brianna went to the fridge to get a juice box, and I gathered my stuff and was about to head out the door, when suddenly she came charging at me like an angry baby rhinoceros in pigtails.

SHE actually accused ME of taking her sandwich!

That's when we started yelling at each other. . . .

16

BRIANNA, ACCUSING ME OF SWIPING HER
YUCK-A-LICIOUS SANDWICH!!

17

"My sandwich is missing, and YOU took it!"

"Brianna! I wouldn't feed that nasty sandwich to my WORST ENEMY!"

And by worst enemy, I meant people like . . . well, you know . . .

MACKENZIE HOLLISTER ☹!!

Although, now that I think about it, I probably WOULD feed that sandwich to my worst enemy.

I'd LOVE to just shove it right down her throat!

Just kidding ☺!

NOT ☹!!

Actually, I really am kidding ☺!

I try to be friendly and get along with EVERYONE at my school. But for some reason, MacKenzie HATES MY GUTS!!

Anyway, by the time I finally left for school, Brianna was busy making another sandwich.

It's like, the older she gets, the more BRATTY she becomes.

I think it's time for me to have a very serious talk with my mom and dad about their parenting skills.

WHY?

Because I'm really SICK and TIRED of Brianna . . .

1. taking my stuff without permission (like my clock!).

2. stealing my cell phone to play the Princess Sugar Plum games and running down my battery.

3. waking me up in the middle of the night to take her to the bathroom, by jumping up and down on my bed (while I'm still in it ☺!!). . . .

BRIANNA, WAKING ME UP
IN A VERY RUDE MANNER!!

It's absolutely vital that my parents get professional help for Brianna before it's too late.

They let her get away with EVERYTHING! But when I ask to do stuff, it's always a big fat "NO!"

I was really looking forward to volunteering at the Fuzzy Friends Animal Rescue Center after school today with my crush, Brandon.

But my mom said I couldn't!

WHY?!! Because I have to babysit BRIANNA!

TYPICAL ☹!!

It was kind of a big deal because this would have been my first time hanging out with Brandon since . . . well, you know!!

My very first KISS!!! SQUEEEEEEEE!!! ☺!!

OMG! I was SO shocked when it happened! I thought I was going to DIE!

It was SO romantic!

Even though my eyes were open the entire time and practically bulging out of my head.

And after it was over, I hyperventilated!

Almost.

The only problem with the kiss is that it happened at a charity event to raise money for kids. So I don't know if Brandon did it because he actually likes me, or because he was just trying to save the needy children of the world.

Anyway, thanks to my KA-RAY-ZEE sister, I'm a nervous wreck and totally stressed out.

And my school day hasn't even started yet!

NOTE TO SELF: Get a NEW sister!!

☹!!

I was happy and relieved that I actually made it to school on time.

In spite of my very cruddy morning, I'd made up my mind that I was going to have a really good day.

I was surprised that my new sweater got SO much attention.

As I was walking down the hall, practically EVERYONE stopped and stared. Even the GUYS!

And get this!! A few of the CCP (Cute, Cool & Popular) girls actually smiled, pointed, and whispered to each other.

It was quite obvious they were LOVING my new sweater!

I felt just like a fashion model walking the runway or something. . . .

EVERYONE STARING AND POINTING AS
I STRUTTED DOWN THE HALL

24

I was like, "Good morning, people! Please don't HATE on my FABULOUS sweater!!" But I just said that inside my head, so no one heard it but me.

When I got to my locker, I put my stuff away and was about to write a quick entry in my diary.

I was feeling REALLY happy about my life right then ☺!

I wasn't even that mad at Brianna anymore. Hey, she's ONLY a little kid! When I was her age, I was WAY more annoying.

Suddenly I noticed MacKenzie staring at me like I was a . . . two-headed, um . . . SQUIRREL or something. But I just ignored her like I always do.

Then she shrieked, "OMG, NIKKI! WHERE DID YOU GET THAT SWEATER?!!"

Which was the STUPIDEST question EVER! That girl has the IQ of a wad of chewed bubble gum! . . .

MACKENZIE   WAD OF GUM

I just glared at her and calmly answered, "I got my sweater from a STORE. You know, where YOU buy stuff, like your HAIR and your TAN."

MacKenzie was obviously INSANELY jealous of my fabulous new sweater.

And she just couldn't deal with the fact that MY outfit was way CUTER than HER outfit.

Then she pointed at me and snickered. . . .

"UM . . . NIKKI, ARE YOU TRYING TO MAKE A FASHION STATEMENT? OR HAVE YOU JUST BEEN EATING OUT OF THE GARBAGE AGAIN?"

27

That's when I finally looked down at my sweater. Plastered across the front of it was . . .

Brianna's missing sandwich ☹!!

I dropped my diary and just STARED in HORROR!!

No wonder I had gotten so many stares from other students in the hall. But, unfortunately, they hadn't been ADMIRING my new sweater.

That's when I noticed that MacKenzie and practically EVERYONE in the hall were pointing and laughing at me.

Like I was some kind of . . .

FREAK!

Then MacKenzie glared at me and snarled, "Hey, Nikki, would you like some FLIES with that sandwich?! Oops, I mean FRIES!"

And everyone laughed even harder!

I could NOT believe this was actually happening to me.

I just stood there with my mouth dangling wide open.

It was like I was waiting for a SUPERclever comeback to crawl up my throat and jump right into MacKenzie's face.

But I couldn't think of a single thing to say to her.

So I just mumbled, "Whatever."

OMG! I felt SO humiliated!

And embarrassed.

And . . . STUPID!

Blinking back my tears, I picked up my diary and shoved it into my backpack.

Then I slammed my locker door shut and took off running down the hall.

☹!!

AAAAAAAAAAHH!!!...
(That was me screaming in frustration! AGAIN ☹!!)

I've just had the WORST. MORNING. EVER!! And right now I'm hiding out in the girls' bathroom.

I STILL cannot believe that huge FIASCO with MacKenzie! And with Brianna's sandwich!

The only logical explanation is that the sandwich probably got stuck on my coat when I tossed it on the kitchen table this morning.

And then, when I put on my coat, it somehow attached itself to the front of my sweater. Like some kind of, um . . . SUPERfreaky, sticky, slimy . . . ALIEN . . . CREATURE!!

I wanted to rush to the nearest emergency room and BEG the doctors for yet another life-saving medical procedure!! . . .

31

"DOCTORS, PLEASE HELP ME! CAN YOU SURGICALLY REMOVE THIS SANDWICH?!"

So Brianna was right. I DID steal her nasty sandwich!

Accidentally ☹!

Anyway, I'm in the bathroom, trying desperately to wipe all the stains off my sweater.

But the situation is hopeless!

I look just like one of Brianna's UGLY finger paintings.

Because now I'm completely covered with:

1. brown peanut-butter stains

2. purple jelly stains

3. white soap suds

AND

4. bright fluorescent-green hand soap from the girls' bathroom.

ME, STARING IN THE MIRROR AND
HAVING A COMPLETE MELTDOWN OVER
THE STAINS ON MY SWEATER!

34

OMG! It looked like someone had SNARFED down a cafeteria lunch of tuna casserole, green peas, blueberry pie, and chocolate milk.

And then THREW UP all over my sweater!!

TWICE ☹!!

I felt absolutely HORRIBLE!

Suddenly, big fat tears started to roll down my cheeks.

But it wasn't because I was SUPERupset (which I WAS)!

My eyes were just burning really badly from the putrid stench of pickle juice. Unfortunately, adding water to the mix had made the noxious odor ten times stronger.

That's when I started to cry for real!

My entire school thinks I'm just a huge JOKE!

My favorite sweater (which I had saved up for TWO whole months to buy!!) was TOTALLY RUINED!!!

AND I smelled like a HUMAN PICKLE with very bad body odor!!!

It was ALL Brianna's fault!! Mostly.

Actually, I don't know who makes my life more miserable, MACKENZIE or BRIANNA!

Thank goodness I had my Sassy Sasha perfume with me. I sprayed on practically half the bottle.

So NOW I smell like . . . (*SNIFF SNIFF*) . . .

A PICKLE marinated in Sassy Sasha perfume!!

JUST GREAT ☹!!

Sorry, Brianna! But I'm starting to wish you were NEVER born!

☹!!

In English class, I slouched down in my chair and tried to hide behind my textbook. The last thing I needed was the entire class staring at my hideous stained sweater.

Soon my English teacher came staggering into the class, carrying a massive four-inch-thick book.

She dropped it onto her desk with a loud
THUMP!

The kids in the front row coughed and fanned the dust cloud it created.

I couldn't help but notice that the ancient book smelled like mildew, fish sticks, and sweaty gym socks.

It smelled as AWFUL as I felt!

Which was a pretty amazing coincidence, when you think about it.

"Good morning, class!" My teacher beamed happily. "Instead of discussing the use of symbolism in our *Grapes of Wrath* novel as originally planned, today we're going to have some fun! So please put away your books."

Everyone happily tossed their *Grapes of Wrath* books on the floor, including me.

Our teacher continued.

"I was cleaning out my attic yesterday and found this awesome treasure!" she exclaimed. "This book of fairy tales belonged to my grandmother and was my favorite book as a child! Fairy tales are an entertaining and fascinating genre in literature."

She picked up the big book and blew the dust off the cover.

Then she proudly held it up for the entire class to see. . . .

MY TEACHER, SHOWING OFF HER
DUSTY OLD BOOK OF FAIRY TALES

"This book actually inspired me to give YOU a
creative writing project today!" she explained.

The entire class groaned, including me.

"Come on, people! This is going to be fun, I promise. Now take out your journals."

I grabbed my English notebook and tried to find a page that wasn't already covered with sketches or doodles.

"I want each of you to rewrite your favorite fairy tale with your own personal twist! It'll be due tomorrow at the end of class. And to get your creative juices flowing, we're going to warm up with a few creative writing exercises.

"A fairy tale is a fictional story that is usually based on folkloric characters such as fairies, goblins, elves, trolls, witches, giants, and talking animals. These stories have their roots in oral traditions, and very similar stories are found in many cultures around the world.

"Every fairy tale has a main character, or protagonist, who is usually a good person. There is often royalty, like a prince, princess, and king and/or queen. Now, for your creative writing exercise,

I want you to fill your journals with ideas for your main character for the next ten minutes. . . ."

Our teacher continued. "Every fairy tale also has an evil character, or antagonist, who tries to harm the good character. This creates the conflict that drives the story. Now fill your page with ideas for your evil character. . . ."

"And finally, there's magic or the granting of a wish. Again, please fill your page with ideas. . . ."

I could have wished that Brianna was never born. But since I'd missed breakfast, I was STARVING! So instead I WISHED I had some FOOD! . . .

"Now let's get started! Try to use some of the ideas from your writing exercises. And feel free to come up and take a look at my book of fairy tales!"

I had to admit, those writing exercises were a lot of fun. I had a ton of great ideas! But I had a really hard time coming up with a story.

I looked around, and the entire room was buzzing with excitement. It seemed everyone was talking about their ideas for their fairy tales.

We were supposed to be brainstorming. But, unfortunately, my brain was farting. I was getting nothing but air.

I've always considered myself a very creative and talented writer. Because, come on, I'm totally addicted to writing in my diary!

But this SUPEReasy, no-rules project was giving me serious anxiety.

That's when I decided to take a look at the fairy tale book to get a few ideas.

My teacher was right! Her book was pretty AWESOME. . . .

ME, TOTALLY LOST IN THE
FASCINATING FAIRY TALE WORLD!

By the end of the hour, everyone was busy writing . . . except ME ☹!

Instead, I had spent the entire class completely absorbed in an exciting fairy tale adventure.

Reading about tearjerking love stories and thrilling adventures was a great escape from my OWN very MUNDANE and extremely CRUDDY existence.

But I still didn't have the slightest idea what I was going to write. I left class more frustrated and discouraged than ever.

I trudged off to my French class, hugging my books, trying to hide the nasty stain on my sweater.

But kids still pointed at me and snickered.

Right now I feel HORRIBLE! Sometimes I wish I could wave a magic wand and disappear!

☹!!

After my French and social studies classes were finally over, I went back to my locker to wait for my BFFs, Chloe and Zoey.

We meet there every day to walk together to gym class. I was surprised when Brandon rushed up to me.

"Hi, Nikki! I've been looking for you all morning. I hope you got my texts! And, um . . . WOW! What happened to your sweater?!"

"What's up, Brandon? I just had a little accident. With a sandwich. But I'm fine. So, you sent me a text?"

"Yeah. Actually, I sent you three. They were pretty important! The journalism camp I'm going to this summer has an opening for a cartoonist. I guess someone from another school canceled."

"Really? That sounds, um . . . interesting," I said, trying to be coolly nonchalant.

BRANDON AND ME, DISCUSSING GOING TO SUMMER CAMP TOGETHER ☺!!

But in the deepest depths of my inner soul, I was literally screaming . . .

OMG! OMG! I COULD JUST DIE AT THE THOUGHT OF POSSIBLY SPENDING THE ENTIRE SUMMER HANGING OUT AT CAMP WITH BRANDON,

TAKING LONG, ROMANTIC WALKS THROUGH THE
WOODS HAND IN HAND, BREATHLESSLY GAZING
INTO EACH OTHER'S EYES WHILE BEING EATEN
ALIVE BY MOSQUITOES!! SQUEEEEEE ☺!!

"Nikki, Mr. Zimmerman said he wants to add a
comic strip to our school newspaper. And he's willing
to pay for either you or MacKenzie to go to camp,
since you're both talented artists. Anyway, I was
hoping it was YOU who signed up, because it looks
like the spot has already been—"

"Hold on, Brandon. Let me check my phone. Now
that I think about it, I haven't gotten ANYTHING
from ANYONE all morning, which is VERY strange."

That's when I took out my cell phone to check my
calls and messages. And Brandon suddenly got this
really puzzled look on his face.

"So, where did you get your phone case? It's
definitely very, um . . . different!" he asked.

"Actually, I got it last month at the mall."

49

BRANDON, WONDERING WHAT'S UP
WITH MY PHONE!

However, when I tried to retrieve the text messages Brandon had sent me, I had two small problems. . . .

First, my cell phone battery was completely DEAD! Which meant Brianna was playing the Princess Sugar Plum games on it without my permission. AGAIN! ☹!!

Second, my eyes were about to rupture and BLEED from the terribly tacky self-portrait she had drawn on my PHONE with a black marker ☹!!!

BRIANNA'S
SELF-PORTRAIT

ME, IN SHOCK AT WHAT
BRIANNA HAD DONE TO MY POOR PHONE!!

But the most disappointing thing was that because I never got Brandon's text messages, MacKenzie will probably be the one spending the summer at camp with Brandon, being eaten alive by mosquitoes, not ME ☹!!

I was CRUSHED! And Brandon was pretty bummed about it too.

Although I felt like crying (AGAIN!), I plastered a big smile across my face and told him how much I appreciated him texting me the camp information, even though I never got a chance to read it because my phone battery was dead.

He kind of shrugged and stuck his hands in his pockets. "Hey, no problem. I guess there's always next year. Right? Anyway, I'll see you in bio."

"Sure. And thanks again," I said as he headed down the hall.

I sighed in frustration and then collapsed against my locker.

It looks like my day is getting CRUDDIER and CRUDDIER by the hour.

Seriously!

I don't know how much more of this DRAMA I can take!!

!!

Good news! I've FINALLY come up with a brilliant plan for how to fix my stained sweater situation.

After gym, I plan to go to the office and call my mom to come pick me up and take me home.

Then I'll take a quick shower so I won't smell like Sassy Sasha and pickle juice.

And after I've changed my clothes, I plan to bury my sweater in the backyard!

If I hurry, I might actually make it back to school in time for bio and get to see Brandon again ☺!

One thing is for sure, I don't know how I would make it at this school without my BFFs, Chloe and Zoey!

No matter how bad I'm feeling, they always manage to make me laugh and lift my spirits. And today was no different.

I told them about all the drama with Brianna, MacKenzie, and Brandon. And then I showed them my messed-up sweater and the graffiti on my phone case. They just stared at me in horror. . . .

ME, SHOWING MY HORRIFIED BFFS
MY MESSED-UP SWEATER
AND THE GRAFFITI ON MY PHONE!

Chloe said, "OMG, Nikki! You poor thing! I feel SO sorry for you!"

And Zoey said, "'When things are bad, we take a bit of comfort in the thought that they could always be WORSE. And when they are, we find hope in the thought that things are so bad they have to get BETTER.'—Malcolm S. Forbes."

Then they both gave me a BIG hug!

So right now I'm feeling a lot better.

Chloe and Zoey are the BEST friends EVER!!!

☺!!

THE PERILS OF P.E.—11:05 a.m.

I could hardly wait for gym to be over so I could finally go home and change.

As we were finishing up our warm-up exercises, our teacher disappeared into the storage closet.

That meant only one thing! We were going to be doing some type of activity with a ball!

JUST GREAT ☹!

She was going to emerge with a basketball, soccer ball, volleyball, baseball, or maybe a football.

Sorry, but I was starving! The only ball I wanted to get up close and personal with right then was a juicy meatball or a savory cheese ball. YUM!!

Unfortunately, my food fantasy was rudely interrupted when the teacher blew her whistle and announced the most HATED gym class activity known to humankind. . . .

Then our teacher threw the balls out on the gym floor and the game began. All the athletic kids immediately scrambled for a ball.

Being the first person out is the ultimate humiliation.

Everyone jeers and makes the L for "loser" sign with their fingers while you slowly do your "walk of shame" to the bleachers.

I wasn't about to let that happen to me!

AGAIN!!

But just in case it DID, I had tucked my diary and pen inside my shirt so I could make good use of my downtime on the bleachers.

I immediately noticed Jessica staring at me the way a hungry snake stares at a mouse. And YIKES! Unfortunately for me, she had a ball in her hands.

Suddenly she took off running toward me.

I bobbed and weaved through the cross fire of flying balls like a pro until she somehow trapped me in a corner.

"Ha! There's nowhere to run now!" She grinned. "Eat rubber, DORK!"

She threw the ball at me, but I ducked just in the nick of time. As the ball ricocheted off the wall, her eyes got as large as saucers.

"UH-OH!" she whimpered, and quickly turned to try to run away.

But the ball smacked her right on her butt!

WHOP!!

"You're OUT! You're OUT!" a boy cried gleefully as he pointed at her.

"YES!!" I shouted in triumph as I did my Snoopy "happy dance" right there on the gym floor.

Jessica was the FIRST person out of the game!!

While the other kids taunted Jessica, I leaned against the wall to catch my breath. Chloe and Zoey excitedly ran up to me and gave me high fives.

"OMG!" Chloe cried. "I thought Jessica had you for sure!"

"Nikki, just take deep breaths," Zoey huffed. "You sound like you're hyperventilating!"

"I'm f-f-fine!" I panted. "But that was close! I thought I was DEAD!"

We'd only been standing there for a few seconds. Then, before I could even scream "WATCH OUT!!" a group of jocks started whipping balls at us like we were giant teddy bears in a carnival arcade game or something.

OMG! We could feel the rush of cool air as the balls whizzed by, just missing our heads.

Chloe, Zoey, and I just FROZE like deer in headlights. . . .

ME AND MY BFFS, GETTING AMBUSHED!

"Well, girlfriends! It's the three of us against the world! And, personally, I think we're DOOMED!" Chloe groaned.

"Come on, guys! Don't give up yet!" Zoey said. "If we're moving targets, they'll have a harder time hitting us. SCATTER! And whatever you do, DON'T. STOP. RUNNING!"

So we took off in different directions, running around the gym like headless chickens.

We ran in circles, zigzags, and swirls. And that strategy really seemed to work.

Because somehow my BFFs and I managed to survive the game. Soon it was down to just the three of us and a few others.

This was the longest we had EVER lasted!

That's when we started to really get into the game. We were running, catching, throwing, and dodging like Olympians. It was actually a lot of fun! . . .

ME AND MY BFFS, HAVING A BLAST
PLAYING DODGEBALL ☺!!

Until MacKenzie suddenly appeared out of nowhere and screamed . . .

"HEY, MAXWELL! EAT THIS!"

She threw the ball at me as hard as she could! . . .

And then . . .

OMG!

I got hit right in the face!!!

It felt like that ball was going one hundred miles an hour.

Suddenly everything was hazy and in slow motion.

I tried to walk to the bleachers, but my legs felt all squishy, like jelly.

Something was wrong.

VERY wrong!

My BFFs' voices sounded really, really far away, almost like an echo.

"Nikkiiiiiiiii!" Zoey cried. "Someone get the teacherrrrr!"

"Oh noooooo!" Chloe screamed. "I think she's huuuurt! Helllllp!"

My head was spinning like crazy!

And so was the room!

That's when I lost my balance and felt myself falling.

Then everything went pitch-black.

☹!!

DESCENDING INTO THE DEEPEST
DEPTHS OF DARKNESS

When I finally opened my eyes, I was surrounded by darkness.

I was completely disoriented and had the weirdest sensation of intense butterflies in my stomach.
It was the same exact feeling you get on a roller coaster.

It actually felt like I was . . . falling?!

YES! That was it!!

OH, CRUD!!!

I was FALLING!!!

And falling . . .

And falling . . .

And FALLING ☹!! . . .

72

SOMEPLACE REALLY WEIRD!!

The only thing I knew for sure was that I WASN'T sure about ANYTHING anymore.

I wasn't sure if I was actually AWAKE and just THOUGHT I was DREAMING! Or if I was actually DREAMING and just THOUGHT I was AWAKE!

I wasn't sure what was reality and what was fantasy.

I was asleep (I think) when suddenly I heard voices.

"Everyone stand back! Give her room to breathe!" said a guy whose voice I didn't recognize.

"Do you think she's still alive?" asked a girl.

"I'm not sure. She looks kind of dead to me. See how dull and lifeless her skin is?" another guy replied.

I was like, Sorry, dude! Unlike MacKenzie, I DON'T have a lifetime membership to You-Pay-We-Spray! tanning salon.

NOTE TO SELF: ALWAYS use blush and bronzing powder. Because you never know when you'll wake up surrounded by a group of insensitive beauty critics who mistake you for DEAD!

"Very good point," another girl agreed. "She looks DEAD to me, too!"

"Oh well! She's lucky the fall killed her BEFORE the Wicked Witch of the West did!" said the second guy.

"Hey, let's check her pockets for munchies!" suggested a third guy.

"Good idea!" the first guy exclaimed. "After all, dead people don't eat snacks. Usually."

Okay, this conversation was, like, way TOO weird!

That's when I suddenly opened my eyes. I was completely surrounded by a group of blurry faces staring at me. . . .

A GROUP OF VERY STRANGE KIDS,
STARING AT ME AND MISTAKING ME
FOR DEAD!

"Not so fast!" I shouted. "I'm NOT dead! YET!"

The startled group gasped and cautiously backed away from me.

Then they quietly whispered among themselves, "She's NOT dead?! Nope! Not dead at all!"

I slowly sat up and looked around. I was on the floor in the gym.

But I had no idea who those kids were.

They were shorter than me, oddly dressed, and covered in . . . what looked like, um . . .

JUNK FOOD?!!

They had candy and popcorn stuck in their hair, chocolate and peanut butter smears on their clothing, and sticky hands and faces.

Those kids' clothing was covered in more food stains than my new sweater. . . .

It was like I had single-handedly started a "sloppy chic" fashion craze.

"Well, dip my chip! She's ALIVE after all!" the first guy exclaimed as he gave me a warm smile. "This is awkward! Please accept our sincerest apologies."

78

"No problem," I muttered as I staggered to my feet, still slightly dizzy. "Ugh! I don't feel so good!"

"I know what will make you feel better!" a small girl said shyly. "How about a lollipop?"

Actually, that sounded like a great idea. I hadn't eaten all day, and I was starving.

The little girl pulled a sucker out of her dark curly hair and offered it to me.

At first glance, it looked like the candy was coated with powdered sugar. YUM!!

But upon closer inspection, I realized it was lint and dandruff!

With a few stray hairs!

EWW ☹!!

I plastered a big smile across my face to keep from gagging. . . .

MUNCHKIN GIRL, OFFERING ME
A HAIRY, LINTY, DANDRUFF-COVERED
LOLLIPOP!

"Gee, thanks, hon! But I just had lunch," I lied.

Then the entire group crowded around and
stared at me as they munched loudly on their
snacks. . . .

VERY STRANGE KIDS, STARING AT ME AS

THEY MUNCH ON SNACKS

"I'm Chip. Nice to meet you!" the first guy finally said, and extended his hand. It was greasy and covered with crumbled potato chips, but I shook it anyway.

"Hi, I'm Nikki! I'm glad to meet you and all of, um . . . . your friends."

"It's a miracle you actually survived that ordeal!" Chip said, with a mouthful of chips.

I quickly glanced around the gym and realized I didn't see ANYONE from my P.E. class.

"Is my class already over? I've never seen any of you before. You must be sixth graders," I said.

What was going on?!

I vaguely remembered MacKenzie SLAMMING me in the face with a ball during a game of dodgeball. And me feeling faint and falling.

Chloe and Zoey had totally panicked and screamed for help and—

Wait a minute!! WHERE were Chloe and Zoey?!!

Had they just left me lying there on the floor and rushed off to their next class?!

Clearly, none of these people were in MY gym class. Heck, I didn't even recognize them as attending my SCHOOL!!

I suddenly felt woozy due to another dizzy spell. Where was the ding-dang school nurse when you really needed her?

And, more important, where was my gym teacher?

Maybe she could explain what was going on. And give me a pass, since I was obviously late for lunch and possibly even bio.

As I slowly limped toward the gym door to leave, it felt like my entire face had been rearranged.

I probably had two black eyes, a busted lip, a chipped tooth, AND a broken nose ☹!!

I was going straight to the office to call my parents to go HOME.

"Good-bye! And thank you for taking care of that evil witch for us! You're our HERO!" Chip cheered as the other students joined in.

I stopped in my tracks and slowly turned around.

"Um, WHAT evil witch? And HOW exactly did I take care of her?" I asked, trying desperately to remember what had happened. "And, um . . . WHO are you guys?"

"Well, we're Munchkins, and we attend Fairy Tale Land Middle School along with all the other storybook characters. MacKenzie, the Wicked Witch of the West, always stole our munchies," Chip explained. "Until YOU came along!"

"MUNCHKINS?! You're kidding me!" I said, glancing around the room for hidden cameras. "Okay! I'm being PUNKED by Chloe and Zoey for some TV show or something! Right?!"

"It's very possible. But I don't know any Munchkins named Chloe or Zoey. Are they Regals, Renegades, or Rogues?"

"HUH?!" I blinked in confusion. "I don't have any idea what you're talking—"

"You know! The stuff we learned in Introduction to Storybook Family Genealogy," Chip said.

"Regals are royalty, like kings, queens, princes, and princesses," said Lollipop Girl.

"Renegades are the brave adventurers who hang out in the woods," said a guy munching on a slice of pizza.

"And the Rogues are magic users, like the witch!" said a girl with a mouthful of cotton candy.

"And the fairies, too! They're the caretakers of Fairy Tale Land!" explained Chip. "Us Munchkins are Renegades."

"You guys CAN'T be serious!" I laughed nervously.

"We're VERY serious. As a heart attack. Totally!"
the group answered solemnly.

My laughter grew a little more shrill and jittery.

For some reason this whole story sounded vaguely
familiar.

Then it hit me!

OMG! Maybe I was in the story of *The Wonderful
Wizard of Oz!*

Only THESE Munchkins actually munched munchies?!!

Or it was very possible that I'd gone completely
INSANE!

"No way!" I gasped as my laughter turned into a
frantic sob. "This CAN'T be real! OMG! I got hit
in the face with a ball by MacKenzie, and now
I'm suffering from BRAIN DAMAGE!!" I shrieked
hysterically.

Lollipop Girl gave me a big hug.

"Don't worry! That mean witch won't bother you anymore. You really gave her a licking!" She giggled.

"Yeah!" Chip chimed in. "You whipped her butt like mashed potatoes!"

"You totally creamed her!" said a boy with a drippy ice-cream cone. "Just like this . . . !"

He demonstrated by greedily gobbling the entire thing in one bite, and then belched loudly.

I gaped in horror, imagining his scoop of Chunky Monkey ice cream as MacKenzie's head.

Sure, I sort of hated that girl a little bit. But I'd NEVER go cannibal and bite her head off!

Although I was pretty sure her head was completely hollow.

Just saying!

"What exactly did I do to her?" I asked nervously. "I don't remember a thing!"

"Well, the witch was standing right here, bullying us and stealing our snacks. Until you fell out of the sky and CLOBBERED her!" said Pizza Boy.

Okay, I DID kind of remember the falling part.

But nothing about a WITCH.

"You were AWESOME!!" Chip gushed. "You landed right on top of her! We actually took pictures. Wanna see them?"

"Um, SURE!" I answered.

He pulled some photos out of his jacket pocket.

"Here's a pic of the witch bullying us. Those wedgies were pretty brutal. . . ."

THE WICKED WITCH OF THE WEST,
BULLYING MUNCHKINS INTO GIVING UP
THEIR MUNCHIES!!

I couldn't believe my eyes!

MacKenzie was dressed in a very fashionable witch
outfit and torturing two Munchkins with double
wedgies! OUCH ☹!!

Chip continued. "And here you are, valiantly coming to our rescue!" . . .

ME, FALLING OUT OF THE SKY,
ABOUT TO CLOBBER
THE WICKED WITCH OF THE WEST

"And then . . . POW!!" Chip shouted excitedly. "You took her out and saved us Munchkins!!" . . .

ME, CLOBBERING THE WITCH!

OMG! It was true! I'd actually landed on the Wicked Witch of the West!!!

I would not have believed that ANY of this had happened if I had not seen the photos with my very own eyes.

"And the final pic is of me and my friends getting even with the witch," Chip explained. "As you can see, I'm really good at drawing mustaches!" . . .

THE MUNCHKINS, DRAWING A MUSTACHE
AND ASSORTED GRAFFITI ON THE FACE
OF THE WICKED WITCH OF THE WEST

OMG! That photo of her just lying there pushed me over the edge, and I TOTALLY lost it!!

"OH NO! I've KILLED MacKenzie!" I wailed. "It was totally an accident. OMG! She's . . . DEAD!! Where's her b–body?!"

"Probably in the school nurse's office," Chip answered. "She woke up right before you did. She's NOT dead. Just REALLY ticked off!"

"Thank goodness! At least I didn't kill her!" I muttered, feeling relieved.

I was NOT a murderer! Woo-hoo ☺!

"Nope! You just ripped her skinny jeans, smeared her lip gloss, broke three fingernails, tore out five hair extensions, and knocked her out of her designer shoes!" giggled Lollipop Girl.

For MacKenzie, suffering all of that public humiliation was probably WORSE than murder!!

That's when I noticed the cutest pair of platform sneakers lying right in the middle of the gym floor. . . .

THE WICKED WITCH OF THE WEST'S
SUPERCUTE DESIGNER SHOES!

I had to admit, those platform sneakers were to DIE for!

"Anyway, the witch was really angry. She said she

was going to hop on her broom and zoom off to the salon for an emergency appointment to get her hair and nails done, right after she visited the school nurse," Chip explained.

"You probably would have been better off accidentally killing her. Because now she's probably going to try and kill YOU!!" a girl with a cupcake said sadly as she wiped away a tear.

"Kill you dead! So sad!" the Munchkins murmured solemnly among themselves.

"Just great! The last thing I need right now is a wicked witch hunting me down. I just want to go HOME!" I whined.

"Well, you could always ask the Good Witch of the North to help you!" Lollipop Girl said. "She's nice, friendly, and powerful."

"I'm going to need all the help I can get. The Wicked Witch of the West sounds like a real drama queen," I said, starting to worry.

Suddenly there was a flash of light, and everyone pointed toward the ceiling. . . .

"Look! There she is right now!" Chip exclaimed.

"WHO? The Wicked Witch . . . ?!" I gulped.

She was the LAST person I wanted to see!

It was DEFINITELY time for me to leave.

Where is a TORNADO when you really need one?

WHICH WITCH IS WHICH?!

I stared in amazement as colorful sprinkles rained down around the room and then disappeared into the air.

I gasped when a little girl appeared, wearing a pink Princess Sugar Plum costume and a HUGE crown. She was carrying a wand that was almost taller than she was.

"BRIANNA?!" I shrieked excitedly. "OMG! I'm SO happy to see you! What are you doing in my gym class? Do Mom and Dad know you're here?"

"Hey, slow your roll, sister," Brianna said, glaring at me. "I don't think we've met before!"

"Of course we've MET! You're my SISTER! Don't you recognize me? You just called me your sister a second ago!"

"Actually, THAT was sarcasm!" Brianna said, rather, um . . . sarcastically.

"Well, you LOOK just like my little sister!" I said, folding my arms and eyeing her suspiciously.

"Sorry, but I'm NOT! I'm Brianna the Fairy Godmother, at your service!" she said, and curtsied. "I also work part-time as the Good Witch of the North on Tuesdays and Thursdays." She handed me a business card written sloppily in crayon. It said . . .

WISHES & ENCHANTMENTS BY BRIANNA

You dream, I deliver—Since 1583

Brianna the Fairy Godmother

a.k.a. Good Witch of the North

President & CEO

(555) 555-0111

Then she gave me a big, warm smile. . . .

BRIANNA, THE FAIRY GODMOTHER
AND THE GOOD WITCH OF THE NORTH!!

"Wow! You've been in business for a long time!"
I exclaimed.

"That's right. I've got centuries' worth of experience.
And I look really good for my age too, don't I?" she
said, admiring her reflection in her wand. "Anyway,
let's talk about YOU! My new client!" She pushed
several buttons on the base of her wand.

Suddenly the star dinged and lit up, just like a
smartphone.

She read her wand and then stared at me as she
tapped her chin in thought.

"Hmm. This says you've traveled to our world from
an alternate universe. And it looks to me like you
were knocked unconscious at some point," Brianna
announced matter-of-factly.

"Wow! How did you know that?!" I asked, amazed.

"Simple. My smartwand calculated where you're from.
The other part was just my lucky guess. OMG! What

happened? It looks like you got hit in the face with a shovel! OUCH!"

That's when I just glared at that girl in complete disgust.

I could NOT believe she was actually talking about my face like that right to my . . . um, FACE.

There was an awkward silence.

Then Brianna giggled nervously. "So, Nikki, what can I help you with today? Anything you want, just ask! However, I must warn you that temporary makeovers only come with a twelve-hour warranty."

"Well, right now I just want to go home! I'm supposed to babysit my sister later today. And I have a really bad feeling I'm going to have a very angry wicked witch hunting me down very soon."

Brianna giggled. "Yeah! You fell right out of the sky, and BAM!! It was HILARIOUS! I saw the video on WhoTube. It's already gone viral!"

"Wait, don't you mean YouTube?" I asked.

"No, it's WHOTUBE!"

"But the correct name is YOUTUBE."

"No! It's WhoTube, Miss Smarty-Pants!" Brianna said, rolling her eyes at me.

"Whatever!" I answered.

"Now, pay close attention! The BEST way to get home is to go to the office. Once there, you're going to ask for an appointment to see the Great and Powerful Wizard of—"

"OZ!" I interrupted. "It's Oz, right? I already know the story!"

"WRONG!" Brianna snapped. "It's the Great and Powerful Wizard of ODD!"

"ODD?! Don't you mean OZ?" I asked.

"No! It's ODD! And please DON'T interrupt me again! If anyone has the power to get you home, it's the Wizard of Odd, also known as Principal Winston. He's got a thick pad of PASSES that can magically transport you anywhere with the mere stroke of his pen. But be careful, because there are also detentions and suspensions lurking around that place. Got it?"

"Got it!" I answered eagerly.

"Also, I'm going to give you this pair of shoes. They have the power to—"

"I know the story!" I interrupted. "Transport me HOME! Right?!"

"WRONG!! They have the power to magically style you from head to toe in one cute outfit!" Brianna explained.

"Oh! Is that all those shoes will do?" I asked, a little disappointed. "I was hoping for a pair of those glittery magic slippers like Dorothy's."

"The Wicked Witch of the West is very vain. HER shoes don't transport. They just STYLE. Sorry!" Brianna said.

Then she dramatically pointed her wand at the platform sneakers.

"Please, everyone needs to stand back at least twelve feet from my wand. It's just a safety precaution to limit your exposure to random magic particles."

Everyone in the room scooted back a bit, and Brianna began a magic chant. . . .

> "Platform sneakers,
> fashionably sweet!
> Find your new home
> on Nikki's, um . . .
> STREET!"

Then she dramatically waved her magic wand, and . . .

Absolutely NOTHING happened! ☹!!

I sighed and tried not to roll my eyes.

Gravely concerned about this recent turn of events, all the Munchkins spoke in hushed tones among themselves.

Brianna, obviously embarrassed, impatiently smacked her wand on the palm of her hand a few times.

"Come ON! I just put new batteries in this thing yesterday!" she muttered.

I didn't want to seem obnoxious or anything, but my guess was that her magic spell was a little off.

"Um, do you think maybe you should have said 'FEET,' instead of 'STREET'? It's just a suggestion. You're totally the expert on magic here!" I said, shrugging my shoulders.

Brianna wrinkled up her nose at me. "I already thought of THAT, Miss Smarty-Pants! So don't tell me how to do my job." She cleared her throat rather loudly and tried the magic chant again. . . .

> "Platform sneakers,
> fashionably sweet!
> Find your new home
> on Nikki's . . .
> FEET!"

Brianna waved her wand, and this time the shoes magically appeared on my feet.

"They belonged to the Wicked Witch of the West, but now they're all yours!" Brianna beamed proudly.

"Thanks! But won't she be a little irritated that I'm wearing her shoes?" I asked.

"Actually, she's going to be FURIOUS! But let's face it. You need them a lot more than she does!" Brianna said matter-of-factly.

"Well, if the shoes won't help me get home, WHY do I even need them?" I grumbled.

"Because your old sneakers STANK! When was the last time you washed those things? They smelled like sardines and baby burp!" Brianna said, fanning her nose.

Even though I was highly insulted, I had to admit Brianna had a really good point.

My mom was forever complaining about exactly the same thing.

Even though I wore them daily in gym class, it had probably been a year since I had washed those sneakers.

I've been needing a new pair of shoes for gym for quite a while now.

Anyway, the new shoes were a PERFECT fit.

And they looked even cuter on. . . .

ME, ADMIRING MY NEW SHOES! (WELL,
ACTUALLY, THE WITCH'S SHOES)

I thanked my fairy godmother for her help and then said good-bye to all my new Munchkin friends. Then I kind of stood there, waiting patiently for Brianna to use her magic wand thingy again.

"Okay, so what's the problem NOW?" she huffed.

"Um . . . aren't you supposed to help me magically find the Wizard of Odd? You know, like in the story."

"NO! But it looks like YOU'RE trying to tell ME how to do my job again!" Brianna snarked.

"Of course not! I—I was just wondering how I'm ever going to find the wizard if I don't have a yellow brick road to follow. Or maybe you can whip up one of those GPS thingies."

Brianna rolled her eyes.

"Simple! His office is where it's ALWAYS been. Just go out this door and down the hall. It's the first door on the right!"

"Um . . . okay. Thanks!" I mumbled, feeling kind of stupid.

Then I turned and rushed toward the gym door.

I planned to go straight to the Fairy Tale Land Middle School office and find the Wizard of Odd. He'd give me a pass to go home, and then I'd call my mom to pick me up. She'd take one look at my sad, puppy-dog eyes, and soon I'd be snuggled in my comfy bed, eating a pint of Ben & Jerry's ice cream with an ice pack on my face.

Yep! I was starting to feel better already.

My day had been one never-ending horror story. But soon my very weird adventure in Fairy Tale Land was going to have a HAPPY ENDING!

☺!!

WHERE AM I?

OMG! I'm totally FREAKING out right now! Things around here are getting more bizarre by the minute!

I exited the gym door just like my fairy godmother, Brianna, had instructed. But there wasn't a hallway outside that door!

NOPE! Just a DARK, CREEPY FOREST!!! ☹!!! And, unfortunately, I'm very ALLERGIC to dark, creepy forests!

I gasped and blinked a few times just to make sure my eyes weren't playing tricks on me.

Then, in a panic, I turned around and tried to rush back to the safety of the gym. But THAT was no longer an option. The door had disappeared into thin air! ☹!!

With the full moon, the huge trees cast spooky shadows that made it even more difficult to see in the darkness.

I felt like I was in one of those scary slasher movies that my parents won't let me watch. However, on a more positive note, my enchanted shoes worked like a charm ☺!

They magically changed my drab gym clothes into a SUPERcute sky-blue dress with a white apron, tights, and shiny black Mary Jane shoes.

Which, for some reason, looked vaguely familiar. . . .

Then it occurred to me that I was dressed just like my favorite storybook character, Alice from *Alice's Adventures in Wonderland*! SQUEEEE ☺!!!

But I digress. . . .

Suddenly I had the very creepy sensation that someone was watching me. As the wind started to howl, I spotted a pair of sinister glowing red eyes staring right at me ☹!!

That's when I screamed and started running through the woods as fast as I could. . . .

I wandered through the forest, totally lost, for what seemed like . . .

FOREVER!

Then cold, hungry, and frightened, I collapsed in exhaustion in front of a huge rock.

How was I ever going to get out of this place?!

That's when I suddenly remembered that I had a fairy godmother.

THANK GOODNESS ☺!!

I cleared my throat and whispered loudly, "Um . . . Brianna! Can you help me? PLEASE!"

But there was no response.

So I tried yelling as loud as I could. . . .

"BRIANNA!!! HELP!!"

But the only response I got was a very peculiar echo: "BRIANNA HELP! BRIANNA HELP! BRIANNA HELP!"

It quickly became very apparent to me that I was in this calamity all alone.

NOTE TO SELF:
Find a NEW fairy godmother!!

☹!!

I took three deep breaths and tried to calm myself.

The last thing I needed to do right then was have a complete meltdown.

Especially since I'd already had three or four today.

I finally came to the logical conclusion that it would probably be easier to find my way out of the forest in the morning.

Assuming, of course, I SURVIVED the night ☹!

ME, LOST AND ALONE
IN THE DARK, CREEPY FOREST!!

So I just sat there next to that big rock, staring
into the darkness, hugging my knees and rocking

back and forth, wishing I was back home with my OWN family, in my OWN room, snuggled in my OWN comfy bed.

And hoping those scary red eyes staring back at me didn't belong to a ferocious animal with really sharp teeth that ATE kids who got slammed in the face during gym, woke up in another world, and ended up lost in the woods in the middle of the night.

Then I finally fell into a deep, fretful sleep.

☹!!

FURRY AND FEATHERED FRIENDS!

I awoke the next morning to the warmth of the sun on my face and the happy sounds of birds chirping.

At first I was dazed and confused.

Why did my pillow feel as hard as a rock? And how did an assortment of furry and feathered critters get into my bedroom?!

That's when all the memories came flooding back into my mind like a tidal wave. I was stuck in some strange storybook land and needed to get back home!

I stretched, got to my feet, and looked around.

The forest looked nothing WHATSOEVER like I remembered from last night.

I couldn't help but smile. I felt just like a Disney princess or something. . . .

ME, WITH MY NEW WOODLAND
CREATURE FRIENDS!

OMG! All those adorable little animals were really friendly. I felt like dancing and singing with them, just like in those sappy movies.

And get this! They even brought me an assortment of fruits, nuts, and berries for breakfast. Which made me VERY happy because I was literally STARVING!!

Yesterday I missed breakfast, lunch, AND dinner. OMG! I was SO hungry I could have chewed the bark right off of a tree!

I ate the delicious treats and stuffed the leftovers in my pockets.

Next, I happily thanked all my newfound friends for their generosity.

No longer exhausted or hungry, I set out to find my way back home.

INTO THE WOODS

One thing was for sure—I definitely liked the friendly, happy daytime woods a lot better than the dark, creepy nighttime woods.

Somehow, I had to find the Wizard of Odd. But I doubted that his office was in the middle of the woods.

I tried not to think about the "what-ifs."

What if I didn't find the wizard?

What if I couldn't find my way back home?

What if I was stuck in this place . . . FOREVER?

About ten minutes into my journey, I stumbled upon a well-worn, winding path and decided to follow it.

I hadn't traveled more than a half mile when I made the most AMAZING discovery. . . .

It was the cutest little cottage I had ever seen!

And it was obviously inhabited, because of the manicured lawn and flowers. I was sure the people living there could help me!

They probably knew the Wizard of Odd. Or knew someone who knew the Wizard of Odd. Or knew someone who knew someone who knew the Wizard of Odd.

HOPEFULLY!

And if they had a phone, I could call my mom and tell her not to worry because I'd be home soon.

I felt really happy and relieved that this whole FIASCO was going to be over.

I excitedly ran to the door and knocked. But no one answered. I knocked again even harder, but still no answer. Then I pounded kind of desperately.

That's when, to my surprise, the door slowly swung open. I poked my head inside.

"Hello? Is anyone home?" I called out.

Since it was kind of an emergency, I stepped inside to have a look around. . . .

SOMEONE HAD EATEN THE SMALLEST
BOWL OF PORRIDGE. . . .

SOMEONE HAD SAT IN AND BROKEN THE
SMALLEST CHAIR. . . .

126

AND THAT SOMEONE WAS STILL SLEEPING IN
THE SMALLEST BED!!

It was a young girl about my age with beautiful curly blond hair. But when I leaned over and took a closer look at her face, I totally freaked out.

"CHLOE?!! OMG! CHLOE!!" I screamed, shaking her awake. "It's me, Nikki! I'm SO happy to see you!"

Startled, the poor girl opened her eyes and sat straight up in the bed, staring at me like I was a lunatic.

"Chloe, it's ME! Nikki! How did YOU get here?" I shouted. "And when did you change your hair?! It's really cute!"

"Actually, my name isn't Chloe. It's Goldilocks! And I don't believe we've ever met before," the girl said as she looked me up and down.

Then a smile slowly spread across her face. "Wait a minute! I DO recognize you! Blue dress and white apron—you're Dorothy from *The Wonderful Wizard of Oz*, right?! You sat in front of me in Managing Dangerous Fairy Tale Animals: Lions, Tigers, and Bears class, right?!"

"Actually, no! I'm sorry, but—"

"No? Are you sure?" Goldilocks said, squinting at me. "Hmm. Now I remember! We were in the same study group for Surviving the Dark, Dangerous Forest: Tips and Tactics! And wasn't Professor Huntsman HAWT? I wouldn't mind flunking that final exam just to be in HIS class again," she gushed. "Right, Dorothy?"

"Sorry, but I'M NOT DOROTHY!!" I said.

Goldilocks stared at me and tapped her chin in thought.

Finally, she smiled again.

"Of course NOT! Everyone was always mixing up you and Dorothy. You're Alice from Alice's Adventures in Wonderland, right? Blue dress, white apron! You and Dorothy are practically twins. I think you and I both had the class Eating on a Budget in Fairy Tale Land: Why Pay When You Can Beg, Borrow, and Steal, and Eat for FREE?"

"Um . . . actually, I'm NOT—"

"And how could I forget!" Goldilocks interrupted. "For your class project, you swallowed 'Drink Me!' juice from that little bottle. Then you grew to ten feet and then shrank to ten inches. It was AWESOME! You totally deserved that A-plus, Alice!"

GOLDILOCKS, RAMBLING ON AND ON ABOUT STUFF AND CALLING ME ALICE ☹!!

Okay, now I was starting to get a little frustrated.
I wasn't Dorothy OR Alice!

"Well, my outfit is kind of a complicated story. I might be dressed like Alice, but I'm really—"

"You know what, Alice, I think you should petition the Fairy Tale Land Council to change your dress color. Now, yellow is way too bright. And green is way too dark! But PINK! That would be JUST right! And then people wouldn't always confuse you with Dorothy. So, do you like porridge? There are two bowls left on the table. I think I'm getting hungry again. . . ."

OMG!! Goldilocks was REEEALLY talkative!!

"To be honest, Goldilocks, I don't think that's such a good idea. What if the bears are hungry too? They might be a little upset when they come home and find all of their porridge gone," I said, starting to worry about that very issue myself.

"Bears?! Did you just say 'BEARS'?!" Goldilocks gasped, looking very alarmed.

"Yes, I did! The Three Bears live in this house!" I explained. "And if I remember the story correctly, they'll be arriving here any minute now."

"Are you sure BEARS live here? I was told by one of the Rogues that this place was a brand-new bed-and-breakfast and I could just drop in anytime since no reservations were required. But now it's starting to make sense. The service is bad, the food is bland, the furniture is cheap, the support staff is nonexistent, and my bed is a little lumpy. As a hotel this place STINKS! Next time, I'm staying at the Fairyott Hotel."

Goldilocks COMPLAINED an awful lot too.

"A Rogue? That's a magic user, right?" I said.

"It was the Wicked Witch of the West, actually. Her name is MacKenzie and she's in my Survey of Fairy Tale Land History class. Rumpelstiltskin is the most BORING history teacher EVER! Sleeping Beauty pretty much snoozes through ALL of his classes. Although, to be honest, that girl snoozes through EVERYTHING!"

"Wow, it sounds like a really fascinating class!" I said.

"Well, it's NOT! After the Great War, Fairy Tale Land was divided into three groups. The REGALS are all of the royalty. They're the lucky ones with perfect lives! And they always get a happily ever after. They have SUPERactive social lives with lots of parties, balls, and weddings. Hey, I'd love to have gourmet food, servants, and a closet full of gorgeous silk dresses and be pampered all day. Most of them are a little spoiled, if you ask me!"

"Yeah, it does sound like they have a lot of fun! I can see why you feel that way," I said.

"The RENEGADES are adventurers. They're courageous and try to help others. That's what I am. But I'm BORED out of my SKULL! If I have to wander through another forest or deal with another mangy wild animal, I'm going to SCREAM! My life is VERY stressful. The insects are annoying, and have you ever tried to get the scent of a SKUNK out of your hair? It's next to impossible! And look at the clothes we get! I've had this ugly cotton dress for the past two years. I'm just DYING to wear a velvet dress with red sparkly shoes for a day. And a Renegade's love life is nonexistent, unless you're really into the outdoorsy types."

I felt bad for Goldilocks. Although, to be honest, she sounded a lot like what I would call a dork.

"And then there are the ROGUES. A lot of them are selfish magic users obsessed with power and prestige. They have no qualms about hurting others to get ahead. And they're VAIN! They love titles like the 'Evil' this or the 'Wicked' that. Their lives are filled with danger, drama, and intrigue.

"The fairies are magic users too, but they are nice. They're responsible for keeping Fairy Tale Land in existence. Basically, we ALL just try to get along and tell our stories."

"Well, I don't know why the Wicked Witch of the West would mislead you, Goldilocks," I said solemnly. "But this place ISN'T a B AND B! And I think we need to get the HECK out of here. FAST!"

ME, EXPLAINING TO GOLDILOCKS
THAT WE SHOULD PROBABLY LEAVE BEFORE
THE THREE BEARS COME HOME!!

Plus, I'm also SUPERallergic to very hungry BEARS!

Suddenly we heard a loud, angry growl from the kitchen.

"Somebody's been EATING my porridge!!" roared Papa Bear.

"Somebody's been eating MY porridge too!!" snarled Mama Bear.

"Somebody's been eating MY porridge! And they ate it all up!" wailed Baby Bear.

Goldilocks and I just froze and stared at each other in horror! The bears were back home! ☹!! Next, the loud, angry growl was even CLOSER to us, from the living room.

"Somebody's been SITTING in my chair!" roared Papa Bear.

"Somebody's been sitting in MY chair too," snarled Mama Bear.

"And somebody sat in MY chair and broke it into pieces!" sobbed Baby Bear.

"Alice, what are we going to do?" Goldilocks whisper-shouted. "I haven't yet taken the class Angry Animals with Very Sharp Teeth: Up Close and Personal!"

"Well, um . . . we can always hide?" I said, shrugging.

"Where?!! Under THIS bed?!! That's the FIRST place they are going to look for us!" Goldilocks said, rolling her eyes.

"YES! Under the bed!" I whispered. "We don't have a choice!"

We quickly straightened Baby Bear's bed so it wouldn't be obvious that someone had been sleeping in it. That's when I realized in horror that I had accidentally dropped some of my personal belongings on the bed.

Goldilocks pointed and motioned frantically, but it was TOO late for me to try to retrieve my stuff.

We were DOOMED ☹! Goldilocks and I
quickly dove under the bed. And when we cautiously
peeked out, the bear family was standing in the
bedroom just inches away from our hiding place. . . .

GOLDILOCKS AND ME,
PEEKING OUT FROM UNDER THE BED!!

"Somebody's been SLEEPING in my bed!!" roared Papa Bear.

"Somebody's been sleeping in MY bed too!!" snarled Mama Bear.

"Somebody's been sleeping in MY bed!" cried Baby Bear. Then he pointed excitedly. "Mama Bear! Papa Bear! Look what's STILL there!!"

Baby Bear's cute little fuzzy toes were so close that his fur was actually tickling my nose. OMG! I was trying my hardest NOT to SNEEZE! I was like, AH! AH! AH! CH—!

That's when Goldilocks quickly reached over and grabbed the end of my nose. The good news was that she stopped my sneeze ☺! The bad news was that the pressure from NOT sneezing almost ruptured my eyeballs! OUCH ☹!!

The bears froze and just STARED at the bed!

"Well, look at that!" bellowed Papa Bear.

"Unbelievable!" shouted Mama Bear.

"LET'S EAT THEM!!" cried Baby Bear.

This is what the Three Bears found. . . .

THE THREE BEARS, FINDING MY YUMMY
STASH OF NUTS, BERRIES, AND FRUIT!

"I have a great idea, Papa Bear!" cooed Mama Bear. "Why don't you and Baby Bear go fix that broken chair while I warm up our porridge and bake us a delicious apple blueberry pie with a honey nut glaze!!" she gushed.

Then all three bears happily lumbered back into the kitchen and got busy with their chores.

As soon as the coast was clear (and the bears were greedily snarfing down a yummy pie), Goldilocks and I climbed out of a window and disappeared into the woods.

I can't really explain it, but for some reason I really like her, even though she's kind of ditzy.

Maybe it's because she looks and acts so much like my BFF Chloe. Minus the curly blond hair.

I'm STILL pretty anxious to go home. But I also want to know more about the ROGUES.

One of them obviously tried to set up my new friend, Chloelocks! Er . . . I mean, GOLDILOCKS!

Thank goodness those bears decided to eat Mama Bear's freshly baked PIE as a midday snack instead of GOLDILOCKS!

YIKES!!

SOMEONE wants Goldilocks DEAD! And that someone is MacKenzie, the Wicked Witch of the West!

I can't even take a wacky trip to Fairy Tale Land without that girl showing up and making my life miserable.

And I'm SURE she's plotting some over-the-top diabolical plan! Which means the Munchkins, Goldilocks, and all of Fairy Tale Land might possibly be in great danger.

And since I'm basically STUCK here in ~~Fairy Tale Land~~ Cray-Cray Land for the time being, I don't have a choice but to try to stop her.

☹!!

BACK INTO THE WOODS!

Goldilocks and I quickly became friends. I told her my story and explained that I was desperately trying to get back home.

Although she personally didn't know the Wizard of Odd, she volunteered to help me find him. Of course I was REALLY happy to hear that news! Goldilocks said it was the least she could do after I had saved her life.

However, first she had to file an incident report with the Fairy Tale Land Council about the Three Bears.

She also explained that a powerful magic user had recently begun interfering with fairy tales and that the Fairy Tale Land Council wanted the person stopped before serious damage was done.

We agreed to meet in one hour at a place called the Mad Hatter Tea Shop. It was located in a small village at the edge of the forest about a mile away.

I had been on the path for about fifteen minutes when I noticed a figure ahead of me in the distance. It was a girl, and she was wearing a bright red cape with a hood and carrying a small basket.

Maybe she knew the Wizard of Odd. I figured it wouldn't hurt to ask.

I took off, running after her as fast as I could. But soon she disappeared into a small cottage.

I was like, JUST GREAT ☹!!

Trespassing on private property was fast becoming a dangerous new hobby of mine. I had barely survived the run-in with the bear family.

However, since it was kind of an emergency, I decided to go inside.

When I finally got a glimpse of the girl, I couldn't believe my eyes! She looked just like my BFF ZOEY!! . . .

Well, okay. IF Zoey was wearing a funky red cape,
a retro dress, cool ankle boots, and was carrying
a cute wicker basket handbag.

Apparently, the girl was visiting her grandmother.

But then their convo got really . . . um, WEIRD!!

Even weirder than the chats between ME and MY grandmother (which are usually pretty weird!).

"Grandma, what big EYES you have!"

"The better to SEE you with, my dear."

"Grandma, what big EARS you have!"

"The better to HEAR you with, my dear."

Anyway, it was quite obvious that Red Riding Hood needed glasses or something, because her GRANDMA looked like no grandma I'd ever seen before.

I don't mean to be rude or impolite, but her grandma was definitely a bit on the homely side.

Okay, I'll be honest. She was a HOT MESS!! . . .

ME, NOTICING THAT GRANDMA
NEEDED TO SHAVE . . . HER ENTIRE BODY!!

"Grandma, what a big NOSE you have!"

"The better to SMELL you with, my dear!"

"Grandma, what big TEETH you have!"

"The better to EAT you with!! GRRRRR!!!"

And with that, the wolf leaped across the bed, right at Red Riding Hood.

Okay, I knew there was supposed to be a huntsman or some guy who shows up at the last minute to save the day in the fairy tale. But he was nowhere in sight.

"Fairy Godmother! Please HELP!" I screamed, praying she would appear. But no luck.

Snarling and gnashing his sharp teeth, that wolf darted right past the door I was hiding behind.

He was about to pounce on poor, helpless Red Riding Hood and rip her to shreds. . . .

THE BIG BAD WOLF, POUNCING ON
POOR RED RIDING HOOD!

That's when I completely PANICKED and did the
first (STUPID) thing that popped into my head. . . .

ME, GRABBING THE WOLF'S TAIL
AND PULLING IT WITH ALL MY MIGHT
IN A DESPERATE ATTEMPT TO SAVE
RED RIDING HOOD!!

But I guess I must have pulled a little too hard or something, because I heard a loud *SNAP*, and then . . .

ME AND THE WOLF, FALLING OVER
WHEN HIS TAIL SNAPS OFF!

151

ME AND THE WOLF,
BOTH VERY SHOCKED AND SURPRISED
THAT HIS TAIL WAS IN MY HAND ☹!

Of course, after the wolf got over the initial shock, he got an attitude about the whole thing. Even though it was quite obviously an accident.

"Look what you've done, you . . . you MONSTER!!" he yelled at me. "I'm lucky to have survived such a vicious attack. You're a psychopath, and you need help!"

"Oh, REALLY?! So I'M the monster here?!" I shouted at him. "Just a minute ago YOU were the one bragging about your big teeth and trying to EAT Red Riding Hood. After dressing up as her GRANDMA, no less! Sorry, dude, but YOU'RE the one who needs some SERIOUS counseling."

Then he got right up in my face, so close I could smell his foul Big Bad Wolf breath.

Suddenly I totally understood how he had huffed and puffed and blew down the houses of those poor Three Little Pigs.

OMG! His breath was THAT bad!!! ☹!!

153

"Listen, Dorothy, if you know what's good for you, you'll stay out of MY neck of the woods!! Or else! And that's NOT a threat, it's a PROMISE!!" he growled at me. Literally.

"I'm NOT Dorothy! And YOU'RE just a big BULLY!"

"Okay then, um . . . . ALICE!! You'd better watch your step!"

"I'm NOT Alice, either!" I shot back.

"Well, you should be! You're wearing her UGLY dress. I personally wouldn't be caught DEAD in that thing, especially with those awful shoes!"

"Hey, have you looked in the mirror lately, Wolf Boy? You're wearing a granny gown with ugly flowers on it, and a matching bonnet. I wouldn't be giving out fashion advice if I were you," I huffed.

Then he rolled his eyes at me, snatched his tail out of my hand, and stomped right out the front door.

ME AND RED RIDING HOOD,
GIGGLING ABOUT THE TAIL FIASCO!

"You actually saved my life! How can I ever thank you, Dorothy?! I mean, er . . . Alice! Or whatever your name is. . . ."

I was totally surprised when she gave me a big hug.

"Here, would you like a free lunch? It's a peanut butter and jelly sandwich. Grandma—I mean, the wolf—didn't eat it."

"I'm really happy I was able to help you," I said. "And thanks for offering me lunch. But after yesterday, I'm just not that into PB and J sandwiches anymore. It's a long and complicated story. But do you know where I can get a triple cheeseburger, extra-large fries, and a supersize drink?!"

"My! What a BIG appetite YOU have!! You could be one of the Three Little Pigs!" she blurted out.

I just ignored that little comment. Something else was kind of bugging me.

"Um, why didn't you realize that the wolf WASN'T your grandma?" I asked her.

"Actually, I wasn't visiting MY grandma. I was just delivering a basket of food for the grandmother of one of the Rogues," Red Riding Hood explained.

"Well, whoever sent you here is either genetically related to the canine family or was trying to turn you into an afternoon snack. I'm really worried that someone is out to get both you and Goldilocks!"

That's when Red Riding Hood gasped and said, "Goldilocks is a good friend of mine! We're both in danger?" Then she clutched her heart and shrieked, "Oh! My! Gosh!"

Someone had actually tried to kill her, and it seemed to be FINALLY sinking in.

But then she blurted out, "MY, what big FEET you have, Dorothy! I mean, Alice!"

Of course I was highly offended by her insensitive little comment. But I figured she'd only said that because the enchanted shoes made my feet look a lot bigger or something.

Anyway, I invited Red Riding Hood to join Goldilocks and me for tea at the Mad Hatter Tea Shop.

Between the three of us, I was sure we'd find that Wizard of Odd guy.

And he'd be able to help me get back home.

THE MAD HATTER TEA SHOP

Red Riding Hood and I met Goldilocks at the Mad
Hatter Tea Shop, a quaint little café at the edge
of the woods.

It was owned by a friendly but eccentric guy,
called the Mad Hatter due to his large collection
of wacky-looking hats.

When he came to our table to take our order,
I couldn't help but stare in shock.

First of all, he had a pet mouse that he carried
around on a small tray, and—get this—they were
wearing matching jackets. (Which, BTW, also shed
light on his name, because obviously this guy was a
little . . . um, MAD!)

And second, he looked just like my good friend
Theodore Swagmire III! Which was not all that
surprising, considering the fact that practically
EVERYONE in Fairy Tale Land looked just like
someone I knew from home. . . .

GOLDILOCKS AND RED RIDING HOOD,
STARING IN DISBELIEF AT THE MOUSE,
WHILE I STARE AT THE MAD HATTER,
WHO LOOKS LIKE THEO SWAGMIRE!

"Welcome to the Mad Hatter Tea Shop, ladies! May I have your order, please?" he said.

"Hi there!" I said. "I'd like lemon tea with honey, and the sunshine lemon cookies, please!"

"Okay! And for you, miss?" he said, looking at Goldilocks.

"Well, I'd like the raspberry tea. But not too hot! And not too cold, either! I think lukewarm would be just right. And, let's see, the peanut butter crunch cookies are too hard. But the old-fashioned tea cookies are too soft. The cinnamon doodles are probably too spicy, and the vanilla wafers too bland. So I think I'll take the chocolate chip cookies! They'll be just right!"

"That sounds good! And now for you, miss?" he said, nodding to Red Riding Hood.

"Well, I have a few things I'd like to discuss before I place my order," Red Riding Hood said.

"Of course. Go right ahead!" The Mad Hatter smiled.

"Well, I couldn't help noticing what a BIG hat you have!"

"Yes, it's my favorite color—green. It was an unbirthday gift from my sister."

"And what a CUTE little mouse you have!"

"I've had him since I was a child. He goes everywhere with me. He loves to nibble on cheese and strawberries."

"Okay, and what a FANCY teapot you have!"

"Thank you! It belonged to my grandmother. I love her dearly. She's as sweet as sugar!"

I was starting to wonder how long Red Riding Hood planned to interrogate the Mad Hatter. But then she nodded her head and smiled.

"Thank you for your comments! I'll have the green tea with extra sugar and the strawberry cheesecake cookies."

OMG!

Our tea and cookies were DELISH! . . .

GOLDILOCKS, RED RIDING HOOD,
AND ME, HAVING A SUPERFUN
TEA PARTY!

Just as we were finishing up, three girls came into the tea shop, accompanied by two royal escorts and five royal guards. . . .

They wore beautiful dresses and the finest jewelry and shoes.

When they spotted Goldilocks and Red Riding Hood, they immediately rushed over and gave them hugs and air kisses.

I was SUPERexcited when Goldilocks introduced me to them. "Rapunzel, Snow White, and Sleeping Beauty, I'd like you to meet my new friend . . ."

That's when I noticed that Rapunzel looked like my friend Marcy, Snow White looked like my friend Violet, and Sleeping Beauty looked like my friend Jenny. I couldn't stop staring at them.

Goldilocks continued. "Her name is—"

"DOROTHY!" the three girls squealed in unison.

"I'd know that dress anywhere," cried Rapunzel.

"Um, no! She's NOT Dorothy," said Goldilocks. "Her name is—"

"ALICE!" the three girls squealed in unison again.

"That dress is a dead giveaway!" said Snow White.

"Sorry, guys! I know the blue dress and white apron are kind of confusing. But my name is Nikki. It's really nice to meet all of you."

The three girls looked at me, then each other, and then me again.

"Hi, Nikki!" said Sleeping Beauty. "We don't recognize your face. What fairy tale are you in?"

"Actually, NONE!"

"Really?" said Rapunzel, with a puzzled look on her face. "That's very strange. EVERYONE in Fairy Tale Land has a story! Have you filed a report with the Fairy Tale Land Council yet? They are supposed to assign you a story within forty-eight hours."

"Yeah, it's pretty simple," said Snow White. "You just tell them if you're Regal, Renegade, or Rogue, and they'll hook you up."

"Well, actually, I'm none of those," I explained. "I ended up here due to a freak accident, and I'm trying to get home. I've been wandering in the woods for almost two days now. So it's quite obvious I'm—"

"RENEGADE!" the three girls excitedly squealed.

"Definitely!" said Rapunzel.

"For sure!" said Snow White.

"Totally!" said Sleeping Beauty.

"LOST!" I said, starting to get a little irritated. "It's quite obvious I'm LOST!" But I understood why those girls said that, seeing as I was wandering in the woods and all.

"Nikki, you are SO lucky!" Rapunzel gushed. "At least you have your independence and get treated like a young adult. When I'm not locked away in some stupid tower going STIR-CRAZY, I can't go anywhere without a royal escort. Why do I need a highly paid babysitter?! And just look at me! Every day is a BAD HAIR day!

I'd love to get a SUPERcute short haircut, but instead I'm dragging around an eighteen-foot-long braid. Do you have any idea how long it takes me to wash and blow-dry my hair? Nineteen hours! I'm a teenager, but I spend most of my time taking care of my hair."

"Don't get me started!" Sleeping Beauty griped. "Our lives are micromanaged by kings, queens, princes, and even witches we've never met before. We're told to do this! Do that! Bite the apple! Prick your finger! Fall asleep! Wake up! Let down your hair! We're really SICK and TIRED of being bossed around. Personally, I'd much rather live in a cute little gingerbread house than a huge, drafty castle. And on Saturday mornings I just wanna sleep in for a few hours. NOT for a HUNDRED YEARS!!! Like, WHO does THAT?!!"

"I'd trade places with you guys in a heartbeat," Snow White fumed. "We're tired of kissing princes, kissing frogs, and kissing seven dwarfs. And if I'm FORCED to attend one more BORING party, I'm going to punch someone! How about a little 'me time'? I'd give anything just to chill out alone in the peaceful woods without some evil hag trying to poison me with an apple!"

Red Riding Hood, Goldilocks, and I just STARED at those girls in disbelief. Who would have guessed that life as a princess was so CRUDDY?! . . .

RAPUNZEL, SNOW WHITE, AND SLEEPING BEAUTY, COMPLAINING ABOUT HOW CRUDDY IT IS TO BE A PRINCESS!

So the Regals thought the Renegades had perfect lives. And the Renegades thought the Regals had perfect lives.

And I'm guessing that some of the Rogues probably felt the same way too.

It appeared that everybody thought everyone else had the PERFECT life. Go figure!

That's when a little lightbulb popped on in my head and I got the most BRILLIANT idea!

"Listen up! If all of you are so unhappy with the way things are, why don't you just change things up a bit?"

"WHAT?!" all five of them gasped.

"Why can't you guys just swap stories or maybe even share them? It sounds like you Renegades would love to go to a party or soak in a bubble bath. And it sounds like you Regals would love to chill out in the woods or go on an adventure. So just do it!"

That's when all five girls started squealing happily and jumping up and down in excitement.

They LOVED my idea!

"What about the Fairy Tale Land Council?" Sleeping Beauty asked. "There are really strict rules about which characters go in which fairy tales. We could get in big trouble!"

"What does it matter, as long as the story is told?" Red Riding Hood said.

"Besides, how will they know?! It will be OUR secret!" Snow White added.

"Well, once the Council sees that the new way of doing things actually works AND everyone is happier, I'm sure they'll come around," I reasoned.

I had a really good feeling that very soon Fairy Tale Land was going to be a much better place! The six of us did a group hug with me in the middle to celebrate a bright and exciting new future. . . .

THE REGALS, THE RENEGADES, AND ME,
DOING A GROUP HUG!!

"Thank you for helping US, Nikki. But NOW we need to help YOU get back home!" said Red Riding Hood.

"Well, my fairy godmother suggested the Wizard of Odd," I said. "But I haven't been able to find him."

"Wait a minute!" Sleeping Beauty yawned excitedly. "Every year the wizard attends the Spring Ball given by King and Queen Charming at their castle. And guess what? I think it's TONIGHT!"

"You're right!" Snow White said. "It's by special invitation to Regals only. But since we're so tired of the royal party scene, we didn't RSVP. So, unfortunately, we're NOT on the guest list. But maybe we can try to SNEAK you in!"

"No! That would be way too dangerous!" I said. "The last thing I want is to risk any of you getting caught and punished for helping me! I'll just have to do this on my own."

After much debate, all five girls reluctantly agreed with me.

We said our good-byes, and then I began the two-mile journey to the Northern Kingdom, which was ruled by King and Queen Charming.

I didn't have any idea how I would get inside the castle to attend the ball. And even if I did, what was the likelihood I'd convince the Wizard of Odd to help me, a total stranger?

The chances of my plan actually working were slim to none.

But if I had any hope of ever returning home, failure was NOT an option!

☹!!

PUMPKINS AND MICE

When I finally reached the Charming Castle in the Northern Kingdom, the royal ball had already begun.

The cream-colored stone castle was even more magnificent than I had imagined. It had seven huge towers with colorful tiled roofs that glistened like jewels in the setting sun.

A least three dozen royal guards stood watch outside on the palace grounds.

Trying to sneak past those guys was going to be next to impossible. I must have looked really suspicious or something, because one of them marched right over and glared at me.

"Excuse me, missy! But the royal ball is by invitation only. So please move along. I don't want to have to arrest you for loitering or trespassing on royal property!" he barked.

OMG! I'd recognize that scowl anywhere.

It was Mr. Grumpy, the security guard from the Bad Boyz concert! But his ID badge said Sir Grumpy of the 5th Royal Battalion.

The last thing I needed right then was to get arrested by an overzealous royal guard. So, I quickly retreated down the castle walkway. And when no one was looking, I ducked inside an open door of the royal horse stables and hid in an empty stall.

I flopped down on a bale of hay and blinked back tears of frustration. If there was ever a time I needed a fairy godmother, this was it.

"BRIANNA! Please help! This is an emergency!" I whisper-shouted in desperation.

I held my breath and waited. But no Brianna!

However, I did manage to get the attention of three horses in neighboring stalls, who stared at me curiously.

I had been hiding in that stall for a couple of hours and must have inadvertently dozed off or something. Because the next thing I knew, someone was tapping me lightly on the shoulder.

I immediately panicked! I thought for sure Sir Grumpy had discovered my hiding place and was about to place me under arrest for trespassing on royal property.

But when I opened my eyes, a smiling face with twinkling eyes was two inches from my nose. . . .

ME, SHOCKED AND SURPRISED
BY AN UNEXPECTED VISITOR!!

I blinked a few times, and when my eyes finally came into focus, I saw it was Brianna, my fairy godmother!

"OMG! Brianna!" I gawked at her. "Where have you been?"

"Sorry I'm late! I got stuck in traffic," she quipped.

"Thank goodness you're here!" I said.

She checked her watch. "Well, I'll be a toothless tooth fairy! It's almost eleven o'clock!" she exclaimed. "We have get you to that royal ball before midnight!"

"Okay! Glam me up!" I cried eagerly. "And just in case there's a cute prince, I want the dress to be short . . . but not that short. And sparkly . . . but not too sparkly. And . . ."

"Shush! I'm the professional here!" Brianna said, looking annoyed. "Just let me do my job!"

"Sorry! I'm just so anxious," I said. "Go ahead."

"Thank you!" Brianna replied as she raised her magic wand and chanted: "Alakazoo! Alakazam! I want a dress that's totally glam!"

With a puff of smoke, I was transformed. I looked down at my dress and gasped. . . .

ME, IN SHOCK BECAUSE MY DRESS
IS MOSTLY MADE OF HAM

I was dressed head to toe in ham and assorted deli meats. My earrings and bracelets were made out of meatballs.

"Umm . . . I feel like I should be served on bread with mayo," I said.

"No, you stupid wand! I said GLAM, not HAM!" Brianna scolded it.

"So, um . . . is this the dress I'll be wearing?" I asked.

"Wait a minute. OH! Here's the problem." Brianna laughed uncomfortably. "I forgot to turn on the voice recognition."

She fidgeted with the wand and then spoke into it, "Testing! Testing! One, two, three! Is this thing on?!"

"Okeydokey! Let's try this again!" Brianna said. "Blah, blah, blah, we want a dress that's totally glam!"

POOF!!

183

"That's more like it! Not to brag, but this dress is _MAGNIFICENT!_" Brianna bragged. "So, what do you think of your new look? Oh, wait. You need a mirror!"

POOF!

Brianna zapped up a mirror.

I gazed at myself and gasped.

"Wow! I look gorgeous!"

I twirled around in my dress. "Thank you!"

"No prob. But we have to hurry! I still have to whip up your horse and carriage!"

Outside the back door of the stable was a small mouse nibbling on a pumpkin.

"PERFECT!" Brianna exclaimed. "Now stand back and be amazed at my awesome power!"

POOF!!

That spell did NOT go so well! . . .

ME, TOTALLY NOT IMPRESSED WITH MY NEW
HORSE AND CARRIAGE!

OMG! Brianna was SO embarrassed!

"Don't worry, Brianna!" I said, trying to make her
feel better. "Actually, the castle is just around the
corner. I really don't need a horse and carriage."

"Are you sure? I probably just need to make a few minor adjustments to my wand."

"Actually, I can just walk. I need the exercise!"

"Great idea!" Brianna said, and tossed the pumpkin pie and mouse over her shoulder. "Besides, one can never get too much exercise!"

I grabbed Brianna and gave her a big hug! "I really, really appreciate all of this. I'm going to find the Wizard of Odd, and he'll have me back home in no time!" I said excitedly.

"Say hello to the king and queen for me! Oh! And remember, the enchantment wears off at midnight, when the clock strikes—"

"Twelve! Yeah! I know the story!" I interrupted. "Thanks again, and good-bye!"

Then I ran toward the castle entrance as fast as my glass slippers would carry me. ☺!!

AT THE ROYAL BALL

I could hardly believe that I was actually going to a ball at the Charming Castle!

Even though my main goal was to find the Wizard of Odd, the thought of hanging out with royalty was SUPERexciting.

As I approached the main entrance, all the guards snapped to attention.

That's when I suddenly remembered that I DIDN'T have an invitation. Which meant there was still a chance I'd be arrested on the spot for trespassing on royal property. Just great ☹!!

I took a deep breath and quickly walked past the guards stationed at the huge doors, all while ~~Mr.~~ Sir Grumpy eyed me suspiciously.

As I entered the ballroom, approximately three hundred guests, dressed in the finest attire, stared at me, pointed, and whispered. . . .

ME, MAKING MY GRAND ENTRANCE
INTO THE BALLROOM

The gigantic ballroom was even more beautiful than I had imagined. It had a towering staircase with white marble floors.

Beautiful tapestries lined the walls, and two huge chandeliers hung in the center of the room, lit with dozens of candles. The royal orchestra played a waltz.

I had been wandering around the room for ten minutes, trying to find a middle-aged guy who could possibly be the wizard, when a young man approached me.

"Excuse me, miss. But I would be most honored if I could have this dance!"

OMG! I almost fainted right there on the spot!

I was gazing into the beautiful brown eyes of a dashing, princely version of BRANDON ROBERTS!

As he reached for my hand, I smiled nervously and blushed profusely. Just like I ALWAYS do when I'm around my crush, Brandon. . . .

ME, FREAKING OUT THAT BRANDON
ASKED ME TO DANCE!!

"I'm Prince Brandon. It's nice to meet you."

"Hello, I—I'm, um . . . Nikki," I stammered.

"Welcome to the Charming Castle, Princess Nikki." He smiled. "So, where are you from?"

I could NOT believe Brandon had just called me Princess Nikki! It was like I was in a fairy tale or something.

Wait! I WAS in a real fairy tale! SQUEEEE ☺!!

"Well, I'm not from your world . . . er, I mean, your kingdom," I answered.

"So, what brings you here, Your Highness? Are you visiting family or friends?"

"Actually, I'm looking for someone. It's a very important personal matter. Maybe you know him?"

Disappointment flashed across Brandon's face. "So, have your parents arranged your marriage?

If so, I wish you both the best. He's a very lucky guy."

"NO! It's NOT like that at all!" I giggled. "I'm looking for the Wizard of Odd."

"Really! The Wizard of Odd? May I ask why?"

"It's regarding, um . . . my travel arrangements. Back to my . . . kingdom. I was told he would be here tonight," I said, glancing around the room again.

"Actually, he's an acquaintance of my parents. I think they said he was called away on an important matter for the Queen of Hearts."

"So the wizard ISN'T here?" I asked, trying to hide my disappointment.

"No. But if it's important for you to see him, perhaps I could escort you to the Queen of Hearts' castle. I'll have the royal guards arrange a carriage whenever you're ready. It's just two miles west of here," Brandon said, staring at me intently.

193

I really appreciated Prince Brandon's offer. But if/when Sir Grumpy figured out who I really was, HE'D escort me, all right . . . straight to the royal dungeon for trespassing!

The last thing I wanted was for Prince Brandon to get into trouble trying to help ME.

"Thank you! I really appreciate your generous offer, but that won't be necessary," I said. "If it's just a few miles, I can walk."

Brandon narrowed his eyes at me. "WALK?! Alone?! In the forest?! Are you sure? Most princesses would never consider doing such a thing."

"Hanging out in the forest can be pretty exciting!" I smiled. "Well, during the daytime, anyway!"

"Well, if you change your mind, just let me know. I could use a little excitement in MY life." He sighed. "There's so much to explore outside these palace walls. But that's impossible to do when I'm always escorted by eight royal guards. My parents insist on it! I'm bored silly of my mundane princely duties!"

"What? No white horse, shining armor, epic quests, or damsels in distress?!" I teased.

"Only Renegades have the freedom to be real heroes. I'd give anything to be one for just a day. Instead, I'm CHASED by screaming fangirls and STALKED by prince-obsessed witches wanting to turn me into a frog!"

"A FROG?!" I snickered. "So, is that where the saying 'You have to kiss a lot of frogs to find your prince' comes from?!"

BRANDON, AS AN ADORABLE FROG?!!

"Hey, that's NOT funny!" Brandon deadpanned. "And to make matters worse, the only things my friends like to do are hang out at my castle, play polo, and party."

"Well, Prince Brandon, it sounds to me like you need to find some NEW friends!" I joked.

"That's great advice. Then it's settled. YOU, Princess Nikki, shall be my NEW best friend!" Brandon winked.

"Well, your new best friend thinks you'd make an AWESOME hero!" I gushed. "You should follow your dreams!"

"I really want to," he said, with a worried look on his face. "But what will my parents say?"

"They'll say they're proud of you! Just go for it!"

The apprehension on his face melted into an encouraged smile.

"I think you're the first person who totally understands me, Princess Nikki! Even though we've just met, you feel like a trusted friend. It's as if I've known you in another life."

"You do! Er . . . I mean, you do . . . seem like a nice guy!"

That's when he smiled and stared at me, and I smiled and stared back at him.

All of this smiling and staring went on for what seemed like FOREVER!

The music started up again, and Brandon took my hand and led me onto the dance floor.

OMG!

Dancing with him was SO romantic. . . .

Practically everyone in the room was staring at us and probably wondering who I was.

PRINCE BRANDON AND ME, DANCING!

We danced and laughed and talked. I wanted the night to last forever.

"I've never met anyone quite like you, Princess Nikki. You're VERY . . . different!" Brandon said.

"Is that a bad thing?" I asked.

"You're smart, funny, and adventurous! I really like you! So, can I see you again? I'll travel to your kingdom, no matter how far away it is."

"I'd love to see you again too!" I gushed. "But, unfortunately, I don't think that's possible!"

"ANYTHING is possible, Your Highness!"

That's when Prince Brandon gazed so deeply into my eyes that my heart skipped a beat!

Squeee!!

Then he leaned in for the perfect fairy tale KISS and . . .

ME, TOTALLY FREAKING OUT
BECAUSE IT'S MIDNIGHT!!

Our perfect fairy tale kiss was rudely interrupted!

"OMG! It's midnight already?" I cried.

I needed to get out of there quick, before I turned
back into . . . well, MYSELF!

"Is something wrong?" Brandon asked, concerned.

"Um . . . YES!! I mean, NO?! It's just that . . .
I really need to be going!"

"WHAT?! But the ball isn't over yet!"

"I know! But I have to go now! It's kind of an . . .
emergency!"

Prince Brandon looked surprised and hurt. "I don't
understand. Did I say something wrong?"

"No! I wish I could explain, but I can't! I'm really
sorry!"

"Princess Nikki! Please! Don't go!"

"It was nice meeting you! Good-bye!!"

"But when will I see you again? I NEED to see you again!" Brandon pleaded. "Please! Will you at least tell me where you live?"

It seems like whenever things are perfect in my life, disaster swoops in like a pigeon with a bad case of diarrhea and poops on my head!

Even though I knew the "Cinderella" story line, I was still pretty upset at the turn of events.

Hey! It wasn't just ANY prince I was DITCHING at the ball!

It was my crush, BRANDON! Right in the middle of a KISS ☹!!

BONG! BONG! BONG! The clock continued to chime.

I turned and hurried across the dance floor and up the grand staircase. . . .

ME, VERY RUDELY DITCHING
PRINCE BRANDON AT THE BALL!!

If you've ever worn heels before, you know that running in those things will almost always guarantee a TRIP to the hospital.

No pun intended!

Lucky for me, I only lost a shoe. Just like in the fairy tale.

As I rushed toward the door, once again the entire ballroom was staring at me, pointing, and whispering.

I was like, JUST GREAT ☹!!

I felt horrible about leaving Prince Brandon at the ball like that! But I didn't have a choice. Or did I?

What girl wouldn't want to be a princess, marry a handsome prince, and live happily ever after?!

I hesitated at the door just for a second and took one final glance over my shoulder. . . .

I felt so sorry for Brandon. And SO confused!!

But he deserved a REAL princess.

Not a FAKE, wannabe princess like ME!

I sighed deeply and was suddenly overcome by a wave of sadness. Then I turned and rushed out the door.

I barely made it past the royal guards as the magical enchantment started to wear off.

Now back in my own clothing, I ducked into the royal stables and made my way to my hiding place in the back stall. I was so mentally and physically exhausted from the night's adventures that I didn't even mind sleeping on the scratchy, smelly hay.

Tomorrow I was going to make the journey to the Queen of Hearts' castle. And once there, I'd convince the Wizard of Odd to help me get back home.

I tried to sleep, but all I could think of was Prince Brandon and the crushed look on his face. I was the CRUELEST person ever!!

Overwhelmed by guilt and remorse, I cried myself to sleep.

☹!!

AT THE QUEEN OF HEARTS' CASTLE

I got up bright and early and began my journey to the Queen of Hearts' castle. I was desperately praying that the wizard would still be there.

I still feel pretty awful about ditching Prince Brandon at the ball. He's such a nice guy.

But the perfect girl for him is out there somewhere. And I'm pretty sure she isn't ME.

Right now my major goal in life is to find my way back home. So starting a relationship with a very cute prince in Fairy Tale Land would only complicate things.

Besides, most of the time I'm totally overwhelmed dealing with just ONE Brandon!

HOW would I ever handle TWO of him?!

Anyway, before I knew it, I found myself standing right outside the Queen of Hearts' castle. . . .

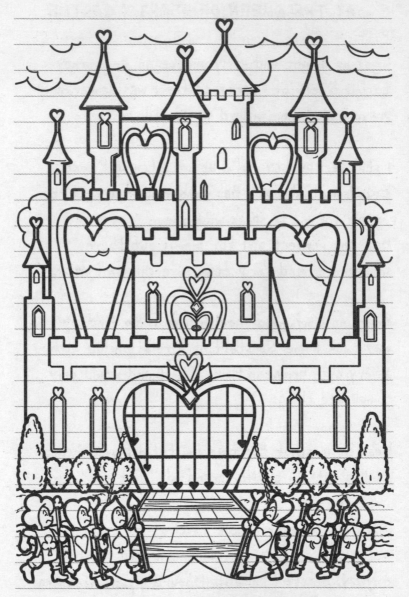

THE QUEEN OF HEARTS' CASTLE!!

It was quite obvious that the queen was totally OBSESSED with hearts! I saw dozens of them! She even had heart-shaped doors and windows. A group of guards marched back and forth in formation at the main entrance. After a few minutes I finally summoned up the courage to approach one of them.

"Excuse me, sir. But I was wondering if it would be possible for me to speak with the—"

"What are you doing out here, missy? Haven't you heard? The Queen of Hearts has decreed a state of emergency! A very dangerous and powerful magic user is terrorizing our citizenry and plans to overthrow Her Royal Highness the Queen. The entire kingdom is on high alert!"

"Wow! I wasn't aware of that! Is the magic user named MacKenzie?" I asked, mostly out of curiosity. "I heard the Munchkins complaining that she'd been harrassing them for quite a while."

"You actually KNOW this diabolical perpetrator?!" he practically shouted as he excitedly summoned the other guards.

"Um . . . no! Actually, I DON'T know for sure WHO the person is. I was j—just asking," I stammered.

"Well, the queen is offering a handsome reward for any information leading to the capture of this heinous criminal. And she's ordered the most powerful magic user in the land to apprehend the person. I think it would be a good idea for you to speak with him. Now come along, please."

"I really wish I could help you. But I'm supposed to be leaving the kingdom very soon. Like, any minute now. I'm really sorry!" I said as I tried to walk away.

But the guards quickly surrounded me.

"It's urgent that you report to the Wizard of Odd for questioning. Please follow me, young lady! GUARDS! FALL IN! FORWARD, MARCH!"

I could not believe my ears! I was being escorted into the castle to see the wizard!! SQUEEEEE ☺!!!

My dream had come true! Because standing inside the great hall was the man himself. . . .

THE GREAT WIZARD OF ODD!!!

I have to admit, I was a little shocked and surprised to see that he looked just like Principal Winston from my middle school.

But hey!

I didn't care if he looked like a two-headed lizard with three eyes, a mustache, and a bad hair weave!!

I was finally going HOME! SQUEEEEE ☺!

I was SO happy, I wanted to cry!

"Hello, Mr. Wizard, sir! I've been searching for you for FOREVER! My name is Nikki Maxwell! And I was wondering if you would PLEASE, PLEASE help me go ho—"

That's when his smile immediately vanished. He narrowed his eyes at me and scowled.

"Did you just say your name is Nikki Maxwell?!" he bellowed.

"Um, y-yes?" I squeaked nervously. The wizard quickly pulled a large scroll from his robe pocket and opened it.

Then he started reading overdramatically in a booming voice, "Nikki Maxwell, Most Wicked Witch of the Unknown Kingdom! By order of the Queen of Hearts, I demand that you cease and desist terrorizing the citizenry of this humble kingdom with your dark and evil magic. Are you prepared to stand before your accusers?"

I didn't have the slightest idea what that guy was talking about. I WASN'T a wicked witch! This had to be some kind of mistake.

"My accusers?! What accusers?!" I sputtered.

"Guards! Bring in the accusers!" the wizard ordered.

A small group was ushered in and stood there GLARING at me. . . .

I FINALLY MEET MY ACCUSERS!

I was a little freaked out when I first saw the Queen of Hearts. She looked suspiciously like the celebrity figure skater Victoria Steel from my Holiday on Ice charity show back in December.

A cold shiver went down my spine. That lady was VAIN, MEAN, and CRAZY!!

The rest of the group included:

1. MacKenzie—Okay, so she was probably still VERY ticked off about the fact that I'd landed on her upon my arrival in Fairy Tale Land. And yes! I was STILL wearing HER magical sneakers (which she hopefully didn't realize because they had changed into a cute pair of black Mary Janes).

2. The Wolf—He was STILL dressed in a granny gown and obviously STILL had an attitude about the whole broken tail thing. Which, BTW, was TOTALLY an accident!

3. The Bear Family—Yes, my friend Goldilocks had pretty much trashed their house AND eaten their

porridge. So I completely understood why they were still a little upset. But I had left them a very yummy snack of nuts and berries. Didn't I get any credit for THAT good deed?!

Suddenly MacKenzie walked up to me, stuck her finger right in my face, and screeched, "YES! That's HER! She tried to brutally murder me! And I think she stole my designer sneakers and is hiding them! She's a very powerful and evil magic user with plans to dispose of the wizard and take over the Queen of Hearts' castle and kingdom. I overheard her bragging about it to the Munchkins! Although she looks innocent and stupid, don't trust her for one second!"

I could NOT believe MacKenzie was LYING about me like that right in front of my FACE!! No wonder everyone was ~~mad~~ even MADDER at me.

"There's been an awful mistake! I didn't do any of those terrible things! Well, okay. Maybe I did a few of them! But some of that stuff was totally by accident. Please, Your Highness. I beg of you! Please do something! Anything!" I cried.

And she did! The Queen of Hearts pointed at me and screamed . . .

"OFF WITH YOUR HEAD!!!"

Then she ordered me to stand trial for my crimes against the kingdom tomorrow at sunrise!!

JUST GREAT ☹!!

That's when MacKenzie came over and gave me a big hug!

"You poor thing! I feel SO bad for you! But, the most important thing is to just stay calm through all of this and NOT lose your head! Oops! Did I just say 'lose your head'? SORRY!"

Then she sashayed away! I just HATE it when MacKenzie sashays.

Anyway, I tried to look on the bright side. I was very sure that by tomorrow the queen would realize she had made a HUGE mistake.

And if I actually did have a trial, there was no doubt in my mind that all my new friends in Fairy Tale Land would testify that I was a decent person.

The challenge was going to be contacting everyone before my trial at sunrise.

Just as I was about to leave the castle to try to round up witnesses for my trial, the guards stopped me.

"Not so fast, Miss Wicked Witch . . . from the . . . Unknown—!"

"I am NOT a wicked witch!" I snapped.

"I have specific orders from the queen to keep you locked up until your trial and execution tomorrow! To the DUNGEON with YOU! You'll be sharing a cell with the rats!!"

"DUNGEON?!! RATS?!! EXECUTION?!!" I gasped.

Then I took a big breath and screamed with every ounce of my being. . . .

"BRIANNA!! HEEEEEEEEELLLP!!"

Unfortunately, Brianna was a no-show. AGAIN!!

Brianna was VERY lucky that the Queen of Hearts had placed me under arrest right then.

Because I would have marched right over to the Fairy Tale Land Council headquarters and filed a complaint against Brianna for "incompetent fairy godmothering" (or whatever) and demanded an immediate replacement!

Anyway, the guards escorted me down three long flights of steps, deep into the bowels of the castle.

Then they locked me in the cold, dark, dank dungeon!!

As I sat on a hard wooden bench, shivering beneath a dirty, tattered blanket, two things suddenly became quite obvious.

I was never going home, and my life was pretty much OVER!!

☹!!

"Get up, you lazy good-for-nothing!!" the Hawk— or in this case, Sir Hawk—yelled as he struck the dungeon bars with his sword.

CLANG! CLANG! CLANG!

I awoke from my nap, startled and confused. Even though I'd only been there five or six hours, it felt like that many days. "What's going on?" I muttered groggily.

"You're expected at the queen's Execution Eve dinner!" Sir Hawk answered as he opened the dungeon door. "Hurry up! You DON'T want to keep Her Highness waiting! She's VERY impatient!"

"Go away! I'm NOT hungry!" I grumped, and covered my head with my tattered blanket like a spoiled toddler.

"You DON'T have a choice." He scowled. "If the queen tells you to eat, you're going to EAT! Or it's OFF with your pretty little HEAD! Got it?!"

I snatched the blanket off my head and glared at that guy. Then I said . . .

"SORRY, DUDE! BUT I'M STAYING RIGHT HERE IN MY CELL! YOU CAN WAKE ME UP **AFTER** MY EXECUTION!"

Sir Hawk pulled a foot-long salami sandwich out of his boot and snarfed it down. Then he burped louder than a large moose. "This isn't a joke, pip-squeak! If I don't take you to the queen, she's going to execute ME!" he said in a quivering voice. "That lady is MEAN and SCARY!"

Even though I was the prisoner, I actually felt sorry for the guy. So I agreed to go to the queen's dinner.

I had originally planned to grab some chicken wing-dings, punch, and cake to take back to my cell. But, unfortunately, the queen had a much more elaborate evening planned for me.

I was surprised to see so many people there. They were dressed in ball gowns and tuxedos, mingling and eating hors d'oeuvres.

The queen was there too, and she was absolutely FURIOUS about something!

She pointed a finger right in my face and started screaming at me like she had lost her mind or something.

ME, HAVING AN AUDIENCE
WITH THE QUEEN OF HEARTS!

"YOU'RE LATE!!" she screamed. "Do you know how BAD you've made ME look in front of MY guests?! How am I supposed to throw an Execution Eve dinner party when the person getting executed isn't here?"

"I'm really sorry, Your Highness! I didn't mean to be late, but I was locked in your—"

"And WHY are you still in those horrible peasant rags?? Have you no SHAME?! Are you trying to embarrass me in front of my guests?!"

"I apologize! But I couldn't shop for a dress even if I wanted to," I answered, somewhat sarcastically. "I've been locked in your dungeon all day! Remember?!"

"THAT is NO excuse!" the queen shrieked. "If you RUIN my execution dinner, it's OFF WITH YOUR HEAD!! Do you understand?"

I nodded. The king, who I could have sworn was my school newspaper adviser, Mr. Zimmerman, sat nervously beside his wife.

"I don't mean to intrude, dear," the king said timidly, "but technically, you're going to execute her anyway. So . . ."

"SILENCE!!!!!!" the queen yelled.

"Yes, d-dear. Where are my manners?" the king stammered nervously. "Why don't I go get you a drink of cold punch, sweetheart?"

"Hello, world! I'm HEEEEEERE!" someone squealed.

I couldn't believe my eyes when MacKenzie sashayed into the party wearing a shimmery black chiffon witch dress and holding a diamond-encrusted gold broom.

"Don't I look stunning?" She twirled around like she was on a fashion runway. "Take it in, darlings! 'GLITCH' is the new 'glamazon'!"

I just rolled my eyes at that girl. "Glitch" was MacKenzie's cheesy slang word for a glamorous witch. . . .

MACKENZIE, THE WICKED GLITCH
("GLAM WITCH") OF THE WEST

I was like, "Sorry, girlfriend. But the only thing glitching here is your BRAIN!" But I just said that inside my head, so no one else heard it but me.

"DARLING! If it isn't the Witch of the West!" the queen exclaimed. "You look amazing, as always!" She walked away to chat with her.

I just stood there alone, scared and desperate to escape. But every exit was blocked by the queen's guards. I sighed and hung my head.

"I'm DOOMED!!" I groaned as I sadly munched on a cold, greasy duck gizzard meatball.

"PSSSSST!" I heard someone say.

I looked around, but I couldn't figure out where the sound was coming from.

"PSSSSST!" came the sound again.

I stared, dumbfounded, at a large potted plant sitting a few feet behind me. Wait! That thing wasn't there a minute ago! That's when a smiling face suddenly popped out of the leaves.

"ACK!!" I screamed. . . .

ME, FREAKING OUT WHEN A HEAD SUDDENLY POPPED OUT OF THE POTTED PLANT

"B-B-Brianna? Is that you?!" I stammered, trying to contain my happiness. . . .

ME, GIVING BRIANNA A BIG HUG!

"Yep," she answered. "You didn't think I was going to just stand by and let you get executed, did you?"

"OMG! I'm SO happy to see you!" I cried. "Please! Just get me outta here!"

"Chill out, girlfriend! Or you're gonna blow my cover!" the plant . . . er, I mean, Brianna hissed at me.

"Okay, sorry! You're a lifesaver!" I gushed. "So, what's the plan? How are you going to get me out of here?"

Brianna scratched her head with her leafy hand. "Actually . . . I haven't figured that part out. Yet!"

"I'm going to be executed in less than twelve hours, and you DON'T have a plan?!" I screeched. Quietly.

"Sorry! But I spent half a day just figuring out how to sneak into this castle. It wasn't easy coming up with such a brilliant disguise. I look like a real houseplant, don't you think?"

"Ugh! Brianna!" I groaned, SUPERannoyed. "Like I said . . . I'M DOOMED!"

"Don't be such a pessimist! Just give me some time, okay?" Brianna said. "I'll come up with a brilliant plan very soon. Trust me! But in the meantime, just try to enjoy your dinner party. You ARE the guest of honor! By the way, congratulations!"

I just rolled my eyes at that girl!

"Anyway, just keep the queen distracted for me. And whatever you do, don't mention a talking plant with pigtails," she instructed me.

"Got it!" I said, giving her a thumbs-up.

"Oh! There's one more thing . . . ," Brianna added. "And it's EXTREMELY important!"

"What do you need me to do?" I asked.

"Well . . . all this sneaking around has made me quite thirsty," she said. "Can you do me a favor and water me? About a gallon should do it."

"WATER YOU?! Brianna, I think you might be taking this plant thing a bit too seriously!"

Just then the queen's butler rang a bell, summoning everyone to the dinner table.

"Ladies and gentlemen, let the Execution Eve feast begin!" the queen declared as the crowd applauded. "Thank you all for coming. The only thing I enjoy more than watching heads roll is celebrating the joyous event with all of YOU, my loyal subjects!"

I swallowed hard and shot Brianna a terrified look. "Who says stuff like that?!" I whispered. "This woman's completely insane!"

"Forget the execution!" Brianna snarked. "You'd have to be criminally insane to decorate with all these tacky red hearts when it's not even Valentine's Day!"

I rolled my eyes at her again.

"Sorry!" she said sheepishly. "Anyway, you'd better rejoin the party before she gets mad again. We don't need her losing her temper and executing you DURING your execution celebration dinner!"

Unfortunately, as crazy as it sounded, I had to admit that Brianna was right! ☹!!

"Okay, Brianna. Good luck coming up with a rescue plan! I'll see you soon!" I said hopefully as I gave her another quick hug.

Then I turned around and bumped right into . . . MACKENZIE ☹!! OMG! I actually peed my pants!

"I've heard of tree huggers! But plant huggers?!" she snarled at me. "What's going on?"

"The experts say t-talking to p-plants helps them to g-grow?" I stammered nervously.

"GUARD! I'm allergic to creepy, sneaky plants like this one. Chop it into itty-bitty pieces and throw it into the fire! NOW!" MacKenzie screeched.

THE GUARD,
CHOPPING UP THE BRIANNA PLANT!!

I've been crying for hours, and I can't seem to stop! It's hard to believe that MacKenzie actually MURDERED my fairy godmother!

Brianna lost her life just trying to help ME! I feel so HORRIBLE right now.

I know Brianna wasn't perfect! But I wish I had been a lot nicer to her. And told her how much I appreciated her.

It's easy to take people you really care about for granted. Then, one day, they're out of your life.

Even though the Brianna plant had been chopped to pieces and burned in the fireplace, I had managed to grab a small leaf and hide it in my pocket.

It was ALL that I had left of her ☹!!

With a very heavy heart, I sadly fulfilled Brianna's last request and watered her.

With my very own TEARS!! . . .

ME, SADLY HOLDING WHAT LITTLE
WAS LEFT OF BRIANNA!

☹!!

Today was my trial and, of course, I was pretty much freaking out ☹!! Sir Hawk placed shackles on my arms and legs and escorted me out of the dungeon. He must have felt guilty or something because he said, "I feel really sorry for you, kid. I hate my job, but I need it to keep FOOD on the table."

I stared at his big, bulging belly. I had a hard time believing he was going to die of starvation anytime soon, even if there WASN'T food on his table.

He continued. "Your trial starts in thirty minutes, and your execution is immediately afterward. They're setting up the guillotine right now!"

"GUILLOTINE!" I shrieked. "But what if I'm found INNOCENT?!"

"The Queen of Hearts is ruthless! And heartless! She'll execute you regardless of the outcome. So it won't really matter if you're innocent."

"But that's NOT fair!" I yelled. "Nobody told me I was going to be executed after my trial even if I was found innocent!"

"What do you mean? I just told you a couple of seconds ago!" Sir Hawk said, looking at me like I had the IQ of belly button lint.

Then he pulled a dozen chicken nuggets out of his helmet and popped them one by one into his mouth. He licked his fingers, burped like an ox, and sadly shook his head.

"Listen, pip-squeak. Being in the queen's justice system is like grabbing a fire-breathing dragon by the tail! Basically . . . you're TOAST!!"

I was DOOMED ☹!! My heart was pounding so hard and fast it seemed to be echoing through the dank stairwell. I gasped when MacKenzie suddenly popped out of nowhere, cackling like a, um . . . WICKED witch!

"You MURDERER!!" I screamed. "WHY?!!"

"WHY? BECAUSE I'M GOING TO BE QUEEN OF FAIRY TALE LAND! BUT FIRST I NEED TO DISPOSE OF YOU AND ALL THE OTHER PESKY RENEGADES!"

"But why the Renegades?" I asked. "What did they ever do to you?"

"They're always hanging out in the woods, sticking their noses in other people's business and interfering with MY master plan!" MacKenzie complained.

"You mean by helping other people, trying to fulfill their own dreams, and making Fairy Tale Land a better place?" I asked.

"Whatever! You sound like a cheap greeting card. The Regals were bored, self-absorbed little brats until YOU came along! Now they're obsessed with becoming heroes," MacKenzie fumed. "It's DISGUSTING! And making my job a lot harder!"

"MacKenzie, YOU'RE a spoiled, self-absorbed, power-hungry little BRAT! And disgusting, too!"

"You say that like it's a BAD thing! It had taken me FOREVER, but I'd finally gotten the Regals and Renegades to hate each other. And THEMSELVES!

Then you came along and messed up everything. So now it's off with your head, girlfriend!"

"Well, if I don't stop you, I'm sure somebody will!" I said, staring right into her beady little eyes.

"Don't count on it, sweetie! The Queen of Hearts and the wizard are already my brainless pawns! And soon I'll dispose of them as well. And your silly, incompetent godmother, Brianna, made a great SALAD, don't you think?! She was NEVER a match for ME!"

When she mentioned poor Brianna, I got a big lump in my throat and blinked back my tears ☹!

MacKenzie was EVIL INCARNATE!!

But I already knew that neither the Queen of Hearts nor the wizard would believe me, even if I exposed her diabolical plan.

"Well, I'd better be going. I have a front-row seat to an execution. And I don't want to keep the queen waiting!" She giggled.

The main courtyard of the castle was packed with spectators and had an almost festive air.

At the center was a huge stage. The queen's throne sat ten feet away from a large guillotine that she had obviously designed herself.

It was heart-shaped, sprinkled with glitter, and decorated with balloons and pink and red hearts.

It was simply ADORABLE ☺!

In a very sick, dark, and demented kind of way ☹!

I took the stage and stood before her, shivering with fear.

The queen smiled and addressed the huge crowd.

"Ladies and gentlemen! Standing before you is the most vicious, cruel, and sinister person of all time. And I am NOT referring to myself! I'm talking about . . . HER!" she said, dramatically pointing at me with her scepter.

A collective gasp rose from the crowd, and a few people booed.

"As your queen, the judge, and the jury, I hereby order that Nikki Maxwell shall be immediately executed for the crime of treason and—"

The king timidly tapped the queen on her shoulder. "Excuse me for interrupting, dear. But what about the trial? To be fair, we first need to have—"

"This is MY courtroom!" she screamed. "And I can do whatever I please! Do you understand that?!"

"Yes, d-dear!" stammered the king.

"But since you insist, we'll have a trial!" she said sweetly. "The first witness I'd like to call to testify is Bud the Baker."

Surprised, Bud the Baker took the stage and stood nervously before the queen.

"So, Bud, what were you doing two days ago, while

Nikki Maxwell was so stealthily corrupting the young people of this kingdom?" the queen asked.

"Um, I dunno! All I do every day is bake," he said with a shrug. "I'm not really sure why you called me up here. I've never seen her before. . . ."

"And what do you bake?"

"Cinnamon rolls. And cupcakes, too," Bud answered.

"I LOVE cupcakes! Do you make the kind with little hearts on them? Those are my favorite!"

"Um, actually, I do," Bud answered.

"How about the ones with yummy cream filling on the inside?"

"Yes, I make those, too!"

I rolled my eyes. What did cream—filled cupcakes have to do with ME? The queen was even more insane than I had imagined.

"Now, would you bake a cream—filled heart cupcake for a ruthless criminal who was encouraging young people TO GO AGAINST THE RULES AND FOLLOW THEIR DREAMS?!!" the queen screamed at Bud the Baker.

"Um . . . well . . . I don't think that would probably be something I'd ever consider doing at the time . . . ," he babbled, overcome with fear.

"Thank you, Bud the Baker! I rest my case! Based on this testimony, I find the defendant, Nikki—"

I couldn't just stand there any longer, listening to her foolishness. So I had to rudely interrupt her.

"Your Highness, with all due respect, I OBJECT to your guilty verdict!" I said. "You're not being fair! And this trial wasn't fair! The people of this kingdom just want to be happy! And all I was trying to do was—"

"Objection OVERRULED!" the queen growled.

Then she stood up and yelled . . .

"NIKKI MAXWELL, I FIND YOU GUILTY OF
TREASON! OFF WITH YOUR HEAD!!"

Four royal guards quickly surrounded me to escort me to the guillotine for my execution.

OMG! I felt like I was going to faint!

MacKenzie was smiling insanely and waving good-bye to me.

"Now, dear! Aren't we being a bit hasty?" the king sputtered. "Surely there are witnesses who actually know what really—"

"Please, your honor! You're making a big mistake!! I beg of you, just let me explain what happened," I pleaded desperately.

"SILENCE!" screamed the Queen of Hearts. "Who among you dares to defy my order of execution?!"

It was so quiet, you could hear a pin drop.

That's when someone cleared his throat and answered, "Your Majesty, I DEFY YOU! Release the princess or answer to ME!"

I couldn't believe my eyes or my ears. Prince Brandon
had come to rescue me ☺!! SQUEEE!!

"The Princess Protectors demand that you free Nikki!" yelled three girls. It was Snow White, Rapunzel, and Sleeping Beauty, channeling the Three Musketeers ☺!

"Let Nikki go! Or ELSE!" shouted Goldilocks and Red Riding Hood! I couldn't help but notice they were rocking glam new makeovers!

OMG! I was SO happy to see all my friends! And from the looks of it, they had come totally prepared to kick some BUTT!

I frantically scanned the crowd, praying I'd see Brianna's big, silly grin. But she WASN'T there. I felt another rush of overwhelming sadness.

Suddenly the Queen of Hearts stood up and bellowed, "GUARDS! APPREHEND THEM! I want them captured alive so I can EXECUTE each and every one of them!"

I watched in awe as the Princess Protectors and Brandon took on a half dozen palace guards.

All three girls were joyriding on Snow White's wheelchair with swords drawn, while Brandon pushed them around the courtyard. They looked like an angry three-horned bull on wheels.

When it became apparent that their side was losing, MacKenzie and the queen tried to sneak away!

But Red Riding Hood and Goldilocks stopped them
DEAD in their tracks! . . .

"GUARD! TAKE CARE OF THESE TWO! NOW!"
yelled the queen.

A burly six-foot-tall guard took one look at
Red Riding Hood and Goldilocks and laughed. "You
two think you're a match for ME?" he scoffed.
"Cute basket! Are you gonna throw cupcakes at me?
I'm really scared. So, what's in the basket, sister?"

Totally ticked off, Red Riding Hood picked up her
basket and swung it at him!

POW! The man lay sprawled on the ground, howling
in pain!!

"OUCH! What was in that basket? ROCKS?!!"

"No, it's the muffins she baked this morning," Goldilocks
said. "They're hard as rocks! And taste like them too!"

With both girls temporarily distracted, MacKenzie
ran toward me as she pulled out her wand. But
Brandon saw her coming. He quickly lunged between
us and threw his arms up to block her. . . .

PRINCE BRANDON, TRYING TO PROTECT ME
FROM THE WICKED WITCH OF THE WEST!!

I was really thankful that Prince Brandon had
stepped in to try to protect me from MacKenzie.
But now he had placed himself in imminent danger.

"Stand aside, Prince Brandon, or you'll be sorry!" MacKenzie threatened.

"If YOU don't back off, YOU'RE going to be sorry," he said, taking a step toward her.

"REALLY!" she sneered. "Well, aren't YOU a BRAVE little prince! But let's see how brave you are when you're green, four inches tall, and hopping around in the swamp eating FLIES!"

"NO!" I shouted. "This is between you and me, MacKenzie! I've already lost Brianna and I don't want you hurting any more innocent people!"

"Hey, I know!" she said as an evil grin spread across her face. "Why don't I turn you BOTH into frogs?! How ROMANTIC!!"

Then she pointed her wand at us. But before we could react, a bright light flashed from a wand and the room filled with mist.

And when it cleared . . .

BRIANNA (YES, BRIANNA!),
TURNING MACKENZIE INTO A FROG!!

When I saw Brianna, I was so happy that I burst into tears.

I gave her the biggest hug EVER! I never imagined that I'd ever see her alive again.

When I asked about the potted plant disguise, Brianna explained that she had quickly ditched it as soon as MacKenzie became suspicious.

The guard had just chopped up a poor houseplant, not Brianna!

Then she'd spent the rest of her time rounding up all my friends to help rescue me from the Queen of Hearts' castle!

Brianna had actually saved my life!

Soon four dozen royal guards from the Charming Kingdom arrived on the scene, and not a minute too soon.

The queen and her royal court were quickly placed

under house arrest, to be brought before King Charming and the Fairy Tale Land Council for punishment.

"Prince Brandon, WHAT are you doing HERE?" I finally asked as he flashed me a big smile.

"Well, after your inspiring pep talk about following my dreams, I decided to go on a very dangerous quest to return a priceless object to the most lovely princess in the kingdom."

"Really? How did it go?" I asked, slightly annoyed.

I didn't want to admit it, but I was feeling a little jealous of whoever this new princess was.

In spite of the time we had spent together at the ball, apparently he had already moved on to someone else.

"Well, actually, I'm not really sure yet," Prince Brandon said, staring at me with a very amused look on his face.

I personally didn't see what was so dang funny.

259

Then he bowed like the perfect gentleman and said . . .

"PRINCESS NIKKI,
I HAVE COURAGEOUSLY RISKED MY LIFE
FOR YOU. IT IS WITH GREAT HONOR
THAT I RETURN THIS TO
ITS RIGHTFUL OWNER."

"My glass slipper! Why, thank you, Prince Brandon!"
I giggled. "And if you don't believe shoes are
THE most important thing in life, you should ask
Cinderella. Or . . . ME!"

Everyone laughed at my silly joke. But I think Prince
Brandon and I laughed the hardest.

It was amazing to see that the Renegades and the
Regals had taken my advice. They were not only
actively pursuing their dreams, but good friends.

Everyone seemed so much happier now than when I had
first arrived. Well, almost everyone! That frog spell
Brianna cast on MacKenzie lasted twenty-four hours.

Soon it was time to say our good-byes.

Red Riding Hood, Goldilocks, Snow White, Rapunzel,
and Sleeping Beauty all gave me big hugs and
promised to come visit me in my "faraway kingdom."

Only Brandon seemed to sense the truth. That we
probably would NEVER see each other again . . .

EXCEPT IN ANOTHER LIFE!

And we were both totally fine with that.

Because EVERYONE knows that in fairy tales the prince and princess ALWAYS live . . .

HAPPILY EVER AFTER!

☺!!

STUCK IN FAIRY TALE LAND! AGAIN!

When Brianna and I met with the Fairy Tale Land Council later that day about my trip home, we received some very bad news. Not a single magic user in the entire kingdom was powerful enough to send me back to another world. Not even the Wizard of Odd!

Actually, the wizard had no magical powers whatsoever! He was a big fake dressed up in a fancy wizard costume, just like in the *Wonderful Wizard of Oz* story.

I had to admit that after the fiasco with the Queen of Hearts and the Wicked Witch of the West, I was happy to be alive! But I still really missed my family and friends and was heartbroken that I'd never see them again.

I was curious when Brianna came in lugging a big dusty book that was almost as large as she was. The weird thing was that it looked SUPERfamiliar.

Finally I realized it was the exact same book

that my English teacher had brought to class!

"So, Nikki! Are you ready to go back home?" Brianna grinned.

"OMG! Brianna, you can send me home?!!" I screamed excitedly. "I thought you said you weren't powerful enough to do that!"

"Well, transporting a person to another world requires advanced magic. But I've been studying this book, and I think I've come up with a magic spell that should do the trick! Are you ready?"

I felt totally torn because now that I was FINALLY going home, I felt a little sad to be leaving. I gave Brianna a big hug and thanked her for saving my life!

"Okay, Nikki! Stand right here!" she instructed.

> "Magic potion, lucky charm!
> Fairy Tale Land is safe from harm!
> Nikki Maxwell saved the day!
> So send her back home right . . . um . . .

"RIGHT . . . NOW! RIGHT . . . THIS MINUTE!
UM, HOW ABOUT RIGHT . . . HANDED?"

Brianna giggled nervously and kept waving her
wand, but nothing happened. I just glared at her.
I was NOT impressed!

Then, out of sheer frustration, Brianna angrily whacked her wand on the floor and shouted . . .

Her wand broke, and the star launched into the air like a guided missile!

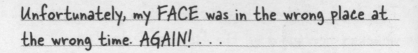

Unfortunately, my FACE was in the wrong place at the wrong time. AGAIN! . . .

I only have a vague memory of what happened after that. . . .

Brianna's magic spell didn't work! But that little
mishap with her broken wand DID!! . . .

270

WAKING UP AGAIN!!

"Look, everyone! I think she's finally coming to!" said a girl who sounded a lot like ~~Zoey~~ Red Riding Hood.

"Thank goodness!" said another girl, who sounded like ~~Chloe~~ Goldilocks. "At least she's not in a coma!"

"Um . . . is she supposed to be twitching like that?" asked a girl who sounded like the Wicked Witch of the West. "She looks like that dying roach I saw in the shower in the girls' locker room! I don't know which one is more DISGUSTING!"

"SHUT UP, MacKenzie!" both girls said in unison.

"You're the one who did this to her!"

"Yeah! You could have killed her!"

I slowly opened my eyes and squinted at the slightly blurry circle of faces staring down at me. . . .

And suddenly I started freaking out! "NO! Not the
WICKED WITCH! HEEELLP!!" I screamed deliriously.

"RATS!! There are RATS in the DUNGEON!! The Queen of Hearts is going to chop off my HEAD!"

My arms flailed about as I imagined a hailstorm of dodgeballs slamming into my face. "THE BALLS! Please make the BALLS go away!"

"Nikki! Please calm down!" Chloe pleaded. She held up two fingers in front of my face. "Just try to focus, okay? How many fingers am I holding up?"

"Fingers? Those look like bunny ears to me," I muttered, staring at her blurry hand.

"You poor thing!" Zoey said, squeezing my arm. "You must be traumatized! But don't worry. You're going to be just fine. Trust me. Now close your eyes, relax, and take deep breaths, okay?"

"Where am I?" I asked groggily. "Where are the Munchkins? Am I still in Fairy Tale Land? Will someone please tell the room to stop spinning?"

That's when Chloe suddenly lost it.

"Fairy Tale Land?! Munchkins?! Nikki, snap out of it!" she yelled hysterically as she grabbed my shoulders and shook me as hard as she could. "I want my old friend back without the brain damage!"

"Stop it, Chloe!" Zoey scolded her. "If you keep shaking the poor girl like she's a Magic 8 Ball, she WILL be brain damaged!"

"Oops! Sorry about that!" Chloe apologized.

"Nikki is still a little disoriented," my gym teacher explained. "But luckily she doesn't appear to have any broken bones. Maybe she'll feel better if we get her up on her feet."

Chloe and Zoey each grabbed an arm and helped me stand up.

"Thanks, guys! I don't know what I'd do without you!" I said, starting to tear up.

"Nikki, we don't know what WE'D do without YOU!" Chloe sniffed.

"Yeah! We were SO scared when you got hurt!" Zoey said, dabbing at a tear.

Then they both gave me a bear hug and gushed . . .

"WE LOVE YOU, NIKKI!!
YOU'RE THE BEST BFF EVER!!"

After a few minutes the dizziness finally went away and I started to feel a lot better.

But get this!

I'd just had the CRAZIEST dream EVER!

About fairy tales!

It seemed SO real! I couldn't help but notice someone staring at me and nervously twirling her hair around her finger. . . .

It was MACKENZIE ☹!!

"OMG, Nikki! I'm so happy you're okay!" she said, plastering a fake smile across her face. "I was SUPERworried about you. It was so scary how you just ran into that ball after it slipped out of my hands! It was such a freak accident!"

The entire class and I just glared at that girl. She was such a liar.

"WHAT?! I didn't do anything w—wrong!" MacKenzie stammered. "I barely touched you!"

"I believe your last words were 'Hey, Maxwell! Eat this!'" Zoey quipped. "Sound familiar?"

"Just shut up and mind your own business!" MacKenzie spat. "I don't have to answer to YOU!"

"But you DO have to answer to Principal Winston," my gym teacher lectured sternly. "I saw everything, and, Miss Hollister, your behavior was totally UNACCEPTABLE! I'm sending you to the office so you can explain your actions to the principal."

"NO! You CAN'T send me to the office!!" MacKenzie shrieked. "It could end up on my permanent record! I'll be ruined! It's NOT fair! I'm going to tell my dad and . . ."

TWEEEEEEEEEET!!

When the gym teacher blew her whistle, MacKenzie finally shut up and stopped ranting.

"Young lady, you can go to the office right NOW! Or you can do it AFTER you run fifty laps around this gym! It's YOUR choice!"

MacKenzie's face grew red with anger.

"Maxwell! You're a total . . . DORK!" she said under her breath as she stormed out of the gym.

"MacKenzie, you say that like it's a BAD thing!" I shot back. "But PLEASE! Don't HATE ME because I'm DORKALICIOUS!"

"She totally deserves detention!" Zoey growled.

"For the rest of the YEAR!" Chloe snarled.

Then my gym teacher called my parents and explained what had happened and told them that I seemed to be okay.

Everyone agreed that it would be a good idea for me to visit the school nurse just for observation.

Actually, I didn't mind.

After everything I'd just been through, the thought of chillaxing on a comfy cot in the nurse's office with my diary sounded really good.

After we got dressed, Chloe and Zoey walked me to my locker.

Then we headed for the nurse's office.

That's when someone came running down the hall, yelling my name.

"NIKKI! NIKKI! I just heard what happened . . . !"

It was ~~Prince~~ Brandon!

He grabbed both of my hands and gazed into my eyes. . . .

SQUEEE!

"NIKKI! I WAS REALLY WORRIED!
ARE YOU OKAY?!"

OMG! It was total déjà vu! Almost like we had shared another life together!

"Actually, Brandon, I'm doing fine. But thank you for asking!" I giggled.

Brandon is such a nice guy! His reaction to the whole thing about me getting hurt in gym was just so . . . SWEET! And ROMANTIC!

SQUEEEEE ☺!!! Chloe and Zoey were practically melting into two syrupy puddles of gushiness!

Of course, MacKenzie had an attitude about the whole thing. I don't know why she is so jealous of my friendship with Brandon.

Anyway, after school everyone was gossiping about how Principal Winston gave MacKenzie a three-day detention for "unsportsmanlike behavior." And as part of detention, students help beautify our school. Of course, no place needed beautification more than the girls' showers!! . . .

MACKENZIE, SCRUBBING THE
GIRLS' SHOWERS DURING DETENTION!!

Even though I didn't appreciate that nasty little comment she made about me in gym, she was correct about there being roaches in the girls' showers.

EWW!!! That had to be the dirtiest job EVER!

I actually felt really sorry for her ☹!

NOT ☺!!

That girl has mercilessly teased and ridiculed me the ENTIRE school year because of my family's business.

But judging by the number of bugs I saw crawling on her, it looks to me like she might need to give Maxwell's Bug Extermination a call!

I'm just sayin' . . .

☺!!

BACK HOME! FINALLY ☺!!—4:15 p.m.

After my fairy tale FIASCO, I was mentally and physically exhausted.

I actually had to guzzle a soda just to get up enough energy to walk home from the bus stop. Otherwise, I probably would have collapsed and fallen asleep right there on Mrs. Wallabanger's front lawn.

OMG! I was SO happy to have finally made it HOME! I guess I've been taking it for granted for most of my life.

The very first thing I noticed was my ~~missing~~ stolen alarm clock sitting on the kitchen table!

And next to it was a sandwich and a note with MY name on it.

I also spotted a pair of ponytails with pink plastic flower barrettes peeking out from around the corner. . . .

ME, VERY HAPPY AND RELIEVED
TO FINALLY BE BACK HOME ☺!!

For some reason, everything at home seemed different.

Somehow . . . BETTER!

I couldn't wait to get back to my own room and sleep in my own bed.

I was even looking forward to seeing Mom and Dad. I planned on giving them both a really big hug just because I could.

And although I had been DREADING writing my own fairy tale, my head was now filled with so many exciting details from my OWN adventures that I thought it was going to BURST!

OMG! I had enough material to write a book. No! A book SERIES!

That assignment was going to be an easy A!

Anyway, I opened the letter with my name on it and immediately recognized Brianna's sloppy handwriting in purple crayon. . . .

ME, READING BRIANNA'S LETTER

Dear Nikki,

Try it! You might like it ☺!!

I wrote this letter to tell you that I am very, very sorry. When you are mad at me, your face looks like Daddy's when he smelled that skunk that was hiding in the garage. And this made me very sad. Your face, not the smelly skunk.

Are you still mad? Pleeze circle one: YES   NO

If you are still mad, pleeze accept my sorryness for taking your clock, calling you a sandwich stealer, playing games on your phone and drawing my very cute face on it, and trying to call ~~Prise~~ Princess Sugar Plum.

I did not reech her. But I did reech a guy

named Moe by mistake, and he was not very polite at all. He said if I reech him again he will call the cops.

That would be very bad becuz I do not think they serve chicken nuggets in jail.

Then I would starve to death, which would not be a very fun time ☹.

Anyway, I made this sandwich just for you because I really care about you. I hope you love it!

You are my very best friend! After Miss Penelope and Princess Sugar Plum.

But you are the BESTEST sister I got ☺!!

Luv,
Brianna

OMG! Who would have thought an apology letter could tug at your heartstrings, bring tears to your eyes, AND make you laugh? ALL at the same time?

It was just SO . . .

Brianna!

That's when I decided to finally give in and try her stupid sandwich.

Especially since she had gone to the trouble to make it for me.

Just a tiny nibble probably wouldn't kill me. RIGHT?!

I closed my eyes and tried to pick up the squishy, gooey sandwich without totally freaking out.

But when I raised it to my mouth, the weird smell of pickles and peanut butter triggered my gag reflex!

ICK ☹!!

"Don't think about it. Just EAT it!" I said to myself as I did a countdown.

"Five . . . four . . . three . . . two . . ." Nervous sweat trickled down my forehead. "ONE!"

I took a big bite and swallowed it as quickly as possible.

"OMG!" I moaned. I could NOT believe what my taste buds were screaming at me!

That sandwich was DELICIOUS!!

I took another bite. And then another!

How was it humanly possible to get all those amazing flavors into one sandwich?! It was the best sandwich I've ever had in my LIFE!

Brianna was still peeking at me from the doorway.

"Brianna! Come here! NOW!" I yelled with my mouth still full.

She timidly poked her head into the kitchen. "Who, me?"

"Yes, YOU!" I answered.

She walked up to me, folded her arms, and stared at her feet nervously.

That's when I gave her a huge hug.

I guess it took her by surprise, because she just stared at me and blinked like I was a two-headed monster or something.

"You're the BESTEST sister I got!" I giggled. "And this is the BESTEST sandwich ever!"

"Told you so!" Brianna grinned.

I had to admit, she was right!

"Okay, Brianna!" I said.

"I will eat it with a DOG!
I will eat it with a FROG!

I will eat it with a CAT!
I will eat it with a RAT!

I will eat it in my ROOM.
On the BUS. And on the MOON!

I will eat it NORTH and SOUTH!
It tastes so yummy in my MOUTH!

Call me PICKY! Call me FICKLE!
I so LOVE PBJ and PICKLES!!"

I fight with Brianna because sometimes she can
be a spoiled BRAT!

But after today I'm actually starting to
appreciate her good qualities. She's clever, cute
as a button, friendly, creative, and she has a
big heart.

But, most important, she's ALWAYS there for
me when I need her!

As a big sister, I'd say I'm pretty lucky!

293

And one thing is for sure: Brianna is a WHOLE LOT
better at making sandwiches than she ever was at
being a fairy godmother. I'm just saying. . . .

ME AND BRIANNA,
SHARING HER YUMMY-LICIOUS SANDWICH ☺!!

Anyway, it's been THE craziest day EVER.

But the good news is that I ended up with my happily ever after!

Thanks to Brianna and all the people who really care about me ☺!

But I swear! If I get WHACKED in the face ONE more time, I'm going to totally lose it!!

Just kidding!

NOT!!!...

I know . . . ! I know . . . !

I'm SUCH a DORK!!

!!

Hey, you!

Wanna take a sneak peek at a few pages of my next diary, *Drama Queen?*

Shhhh! It's a secret. . . .

WEDNESDAY, APRIL 2

The past twenty-four hours of my life have been so disgustingly NAUSEATING that I'm actually starting to feel like a . . . puddle of . . . um, cat . . . VOMIT!!

First I ruined my brand-new sweater with a PBJ and pickle sandwich (a long story).

Then I got hit in the face by a dodgeball during gym in front of the ENTIRE class and ended up trapped in a wacky fairy tale (an even longer story!).

Okay, I can handle the utter HUMILIATION of walking around school OBLIVIOUS to the fact that a SANDWICH is stuck to my abdomen like duct tape.

Hey, I can even handle a mild concussion. However, what I CAN'T handle is the fact that "someone" started an AWFUL rumor about me!

I overheard two CCP (Cute, Cool & Popular) girls gossiping about it in the bathroom.

Rumor has it that my CRUSH kissed me (at a charity event last weekend) on a DARE merely to snag a FREE large pizza from Queasy Cheesy!

Of course I totally FREAKED when I heard it! Not only is a dare like that rude and insensitive, but it's a very cruel joke to play on a person like . . . well . . . ME!

I was SURE the whole thing was a big fat LIE! Sorry! But everyone knows Queasy Cheesy pizzas are just NASTY! Had it been a dare for a yummy Crazy Burger, I'd TOTALLY believe it!

Hey, I'll be the first to admit, that rumor could have been A LOT worse. But STILL . . . !! I just wish "someone" would stay out of my personal business. And by "someone," I mean my mortal enemy . . . MACKENZIE HOLLISTER ☹!!

I don't know why that girl HATES MY GUTS! It wasn't MY fault Principal Winston gave her a three-day detention for "unsportsmanlike behavior" for slamming me in the face with that dodgeball.

I'm really LUCKY I'm not in a COMA right now!
Or undergoing life-threatening surgery . . .

Anyway, as punishment for what MacKenzie did to me, she has to clean the bug-infested showers in the girls' locker room.

Unfortunately, I learned today that the bug problem in there is REALLY bad!!

I was sitting behind MacKenzie in French class finishing up my homework when I noticed there was something stuck in her hair.

At first I thought it was one of those fancy designer barrettes she loves to wear. But when I took a closer look, I realized it was actually a gigantic dead STINK BUG!! EWW ☹!!

That's when I tapped her on the shoulder. "Um, MacKenzie! Excuse me, but I just wanted to let you know that—"

"Nikki, WHY are you even talking to me?! Just mind your OWN business!" she said, glaring at me like I was something her spoiled poodle, Fifi, had left in the grass in her backyard.

MACKENZIE, GLARING AT ME
IN A VERY RUDE MANNER!

"Okay! Then I won't tell you there's a huge dead STINK BUG in your hair!" I said very calmly. "Besides, it kinda looks like an ugly barrette! And it totally complements your eye color!"

"WHAT?!" MacKenzie gasped, and her eyes got as big as saucers.

She whipped out her makeup mirror.

"OMG! OMG! There's a big black . . . INSECT with prickly legs tangled in my golden tresses! EEEEEEEEEEEK!!!" she shrieked. Then she started jumping around hysterically and shaking her hair to get it out. She had a complete meltdown!

"You're making it worse. Now it's even more tangled in there. Just sit down and chillax!" I said as I grabbed a tissue and reached for her hair.

"GET AWAY FROM ME!!" she screamed. "I don't want TWO disgusting CREATURES in my beautiful hair!"

"Stop acting like a spoiled BRAT!" I shot back.
I'm just removing the bug for you! See?!"

ME, REMOVING THE STINK BUG
FROM MACKENZIE'S HAIR

"That is DISGUSTING! Get it away from me!"

"You're welcome!" I said, glaring at her.

"Hmph! Don't expect a thank-you from me! It's all YOUR fault that bug was in my hair! It's probably from those nasty showers I'm being forced to clean."

Suddenly she folded her arms and narrowed her eyes at me.

"Or maybe YOU put it in my hair to try to ruin my reputation! I bet you want everyone to think my house is overrun with disgusting bugs! Again."

"MacKenzie, I think your lip gloss must be leaking into your brain. That's ridiculous!"

"How could you put that nasty BUG in my hair?! I'm getting SICK just thinking about it. UGH!!"

Then she covered her mouth and mumbled something. But I couldn't understand a word. . . .

ME, TRYING TO FIGURE OUT WHAT
MACKENZIE WAS SAYING!

Although we were in French class, it definitely
didn't sound like she was speaking French!

By the time I FINALLY figured out what she was saying, it was TOO late.

Desperate, she took off running toward the wastebasket at the front of the room.

But, unfortunately, she DIDN'T make it.

I could NOT believe that MacKenzie Hollister, the QUEEN of the CCPs, actually threw up in front of the ENTIRE French class!

She was like a bad car accident! I really DIDN'T want to see her covered in puke from head to toe ☹! But I couldn't help staring ☺!

I have never seen her SO embarrassed. SO humiliated. SO vulnerable. SO um . . . MESSY!

I was both shocked and surprised when I was suddenly overcome with overwhelming emotion.

I had NEVER, EVER felt more SORRY for a human being in my ENTIRE life! . . .

Don't miss more diaries

Dork Diaries

**Dork Diaries:
Party Time**

**Dork Diaries:
Pop Star**

**Dork Diaries:
Skating Sensation**

**Dork Diaries:
Dear Dork**

**Dork Diaries:
Holiday Heartbreak**

by Rachel Renée Russell!

MOST IMPORTANT TIP EVER FROM NIKKI MAXWELL:

Always let your inner DORK shine through!

#1 New York Times Bestselling Series

**Dork Diaries:
TV Star**

**Dork Diaries:
Once Upon a Dork**

**Dork Diaries:
Drama Queen**

**Dork Diaries:
Puppy Love**

**Dork Diaries:
OMG! All About
Me Diary**

**Dork Diaries:
How to Dork
Your Diary**

Rachel Renée Russell is the #1 *New York Times* bestselling author of the block-buster book series Dork Diaries and the exciting new series The Misadventures of Max Crumbly.

There are more than twenty-five million copies of her books in print worldwide, and they have been translated into thirty-six languages.

She enjoys working with her two daughters, Erin and Nikki, who help write and illustrate her books.

Rachel's message is "Become the hero you've always admired!"